TRY ME

TRY ME

RIKKI DIXON

URBAN BOOKS

www.urbanbooks.net

This is a work of fiction. Any references or similarities to actual events, real people, living or dead, or to real locales are intended to give the novel a sense of reality. Any similarity in other names, characters, places, and incidents is entirely coincidental.

URBAN SOUL is published by

Urban Books
10 Brennan Place
Deer Park, NY 11729

ISBN-13: 978-1-59983-072-8
ISBN-10: 1-59983-072-8

First Printing: August 2009
10 9 8 7 6 5 4 3 2 1

Printed in the United States of America

TRY ME

The Cadillac Escalade stopped in front of the two-story brick house in the trendy Lakes of Parkway subdivision, in one of the most exclusive neighborhoods in west Houston. The Escalade's sleek black door opened, and a slim, fishnetted, stiletto-clad leg slowly eased out. By the time Tamara stepped out of the SUV, a suave Leon Swanson strolled out onto the patio to greet her. He walked down three steps and stood near the opened door. His gaze traveled from her feet to her head before he took her hand into his.

Tamara had been blindfolded for the trip, but she didn't mind. She had been working nearly thirty days to get this close to Leon. The invitation to his home alone was well worth all of the work.

"Okay, that'll be it for the night." Tamara heard Leon say to the driver, who was responsible for delivering her safely. She liked the way he did things—he wasn't shy about spreading his power or wealth around.

"We'll take that off as soon as we get inside," Leon said.

Tamara listened to the gravel crunch beneath the truck's tires as the driver took off.

Even in semidarkness, Tamara's beauty stood out. She was a pecan color, with an oval-shaped face. She paid for the permanent eyeliner that gave her almond-shaped eyes a finished appearance at all times. Her full lips looked naturally lined, and she had a beauty mark just beneath her right nostril. Sometimes she switched it to the left, but the right side had become sort of her trademark. Tamara was tall, thanks to the four-inch heels she damn near slept in. She was slim, thanks to the rigorous workout she did religiously four days a week. And she needed a slim, tight body for times just like these. Tamara stood silently inside the foyer, waiting for Leon to remove the blindfold from her eyes.

She didn't know why he felt the need to go through all this so-called security anyway. If someone really wanted to find him, they would, just as she had. But Leon was known for being cautious. He said he didn't like anybody at his house; he had even rented a car service just to bring Tamara up for the night. A few minutes later, with blindfold removed, she stood, freezing, at the entry to his living room. Leon had turned the air down because it was hot and humid in Houston, even at two in the morning. Tamara gazed around the room, trying to act unimpressed as she took in her surroundings.

The first thing to catch her eye was the open stairway, which stretched the entire length of the second floor. There was a cascading staircase near the foyer. A large leather sectional sat to her right, but it still didn't take up a lot of space. The massive plasma-screen TV, which hung directly across from it, nearly made her lose her breath.

When Leon walked away from the eight-foot mahogany door and past her, she smelled his lingering cologne.

Hmmm, he sure knows how to do it. The Cristal, the seafood on ice, and music playing in the background. He even has the nerve to have his double-sided fireplace burning.

Leon was larger than life, known for doing things real big. He stretched back on his Italian leather sofa, his fingers laced behind the back of his head. Tamara didn't hesitate to drop her trench coat in a grand way. Wearing only a black lace thong and matching pushup bra, she tried to act indifferent to the surroundings that stretched out before her eyes.

"Hmm, Victoria's Secret fall catalog, page sixty-five," Leon said, sucking his teeth.

"All for you, Daddy. You see, I know exactly what you like." Tamara strutted in front of Leon, making sure his eyes took in every nook and cranny of her goddess of a body. Before she turned to face him, she tried to glance at the clock in the dining room.

She didn't want to appear too anxious, but the juices from her coochie had already started a trail down her inner thigh. She'd fuck Leon if she had to, make no mistake about it—this was all business, as far as Tamara was concerned. Leon looked like he had died and gone to heaven, even though Tamara hadn't even laid a finger on his body yet.

Leon wasn't a big man; he stood a mere five feet six inches tall. He wasn't bulky, but you could tell he lived well. He wasn't sporting no beer belly either.

Leon kept his fingers manicured, his feet as clean and nice as a female's, and was always groomed. One thing for sure, Tamara liked his style.

"Come here, Ma. Daddy got something real nice for you," Leon crooned.

"And I want it too. I want all of it." Tamara waltzed over to the couch near Leon. She gazed down at his crotch and saw just how excited he was about her little performance. Tamara dropped down to her knees and spread his legs open. She used her hand to stroke his stiff dick through his pants. She shoved his shirt up and planted a trail of wet kisses all around his navel.

Leon eased his head back in sheer ecstasy. "Oh, girl, shit, that's what I'm talking about." He used his hand to stroke her shoulder-length auburn curls. Tamara eased beyond his reach. She didn't want her wig to come off, not that it ever had while she was getting busy, but she didn't need to take any chances.

Tamara reached her hand into his pants and stroked him again. His flesh felt good and hot in the palm of her hand. When he released a growling moan, Tamara glanced toward the clock and then the door.

"C'mon, lick it, girl," Leon said, moaning.

"You want me to lick it, Daddy?" Tamara asked breathlessly.

"Emm-hmm," Leon moaned again.

"Ah, you—you want me to lick it for you, Daa-ddy?"

"C'mon, girl. You got a brotha in pain over here, it's time for some real action," he pleaded.

A girl's gotta do what a girl's gotta do. She smiled

as Leon's eyes rolled up into the back of his head, just from the hand action alone.

Just as Tamara had made up her mind to deep throat Leon, the front door was suddenly smashed off its hinges.

"Don't move and you won't get hurt!" the husky voice screamed.

Tamara jumped, screamed, then crawled up onto the sofa. "Oh, my God, what the fuck is going on! Leee-oon!" she screamed.

Leon couldn't catch his bearings fast enough; he looked around as the masked gunmen rushed into the room.

"C'mon, nigga, you know what we want. Get your ass up!" the stocky one shouted.

"Oh shit! What the fuck? What the fuck," Tamara screamed, shivering as she reached for a pillow to cover her naked body. "Leee-on," she cried.

"If you don't shut the fuck up, I'ma blast a hole through your fucking head," the skinny one said, holding a sawed-off shotgun to Tamara's head.

Tamara's heart nearly stopped. The tears forming in her eyes froze and pooled, but they didn't dare fall.

"Man, y'all making a mistake, you don't know who you fuckin' wit, young buck." Leon eyed the gunman closely.

"Nigga, if you don't get up and get what the fuck we want, you gon' be that dead nigga. Old head!" He nudged Leon in the chest with his shotgun. "Now c'mon, we ain't got all day."

"The safe, nigga, the safe," the gunman at the door yelled.

Reluctantly Leon eased up off the couch. He looked at Tamara, who had her head buried in the palm of her hands. "I'ma take care of this, don't worry," he assured her.

"I just wanna go home," she cried.

"Yo! You ain't goin' nowhere! You need to shut the fuck up, I ain't gonna tell you again. Crying bitches don't do nothing but make me nervous. And when I get nervous, my fingers get to twitchin'," he said.

The gunman standing near Leon pulled out a large duffel bag. "C'mon, let's go, nigga'."

"Yeah, fill that bitch up, or you's a dead-ass nigga," the man at the door screamed.

Nearly an hour later, Leon was screaming as he spoke on the phone.

"I don't know who them fools are, but they done robbed the wrong motherfucka! That shit was foul. Look, round up the cavalry, I need a line on them niggas."

Tamara sat in the corner, wrapped tightly in her trench coat. She had been ready to go the minute the gunmen ran out of the house. But Leon had asked, no, told her to stay put. She didn't have time for this kind of shit. She sat back and watched as he ranted and raved all around the house, cussing and fussing about how them niggas jacked him up.

He tried to say the money wasn't nothing, but if that was truly the case, Tamara felt like he would've dropped it long ago.

"It's the motherfuckin' principle!" he screamed

into the phone. "Niggas in H-town know I'm that nigga, and I ain't to be fucked with!"

Tamara rolled her eyes and pulled the band around the waist of her trench coat. She didn't care if she ever laid eyes on Leon again. She just wanted out.

Target: Bobby McNeal, aka Gin
Holdings: numerous successful drug houses in Houston, owns four spas and two adult-video stores, silent partner in Pleasures Gentleman's Club, 2004 big-body Benz, BMW SUV, Porsche
Estimated street net worth: 10 million
Drop schedule: the 16th & 2nd monthly (in addition to offshore accounts), lots of cash, doesn't trust banks
Security detail: travels with entourage, no known address, moves around regularly
Weakness: women with light-colored hair, loves visiting gentlemen's clubs, blow jobs, Hennessy on the rocks
Misc: never seen during the day, fear of heights, anal-sex fetish

Nikki had been standing in the lobby of Pleasures Gentleman's Club, off Westheimer, for about an hour. She was becoming restless. "I'll bet they make a grip in this mug," she said aloud as she looked around the club.

Nearly twenty minutes after that thought, her cell phone rang. "Yeah?" she said, closely eyeing every man who walked through the doors.

"He just pulled up," Marleeta said.

"Damn, it's about time. I was getting tired of holding up the wall in this mug," Nikki said.

"'Kay, get to work. Call if you need anything," Marleeta said before Nikki pressed the end button on her cell phone.

She quickly dropped the cell phone into her Prada bag and rushed off to the ladies' room. She made sure her makeup was just right. Nikki was sporting a platinum blond wig with a fierce pageboy haircut. She had on a black spandex bodysuit that made her ass look even bigger than it was. The "come fuck me" heels polished off her look. Confident that she had waited long enough, she rushed out of the ladies' room and grabbed the first waitress she bumped into.

Nikki produced a one-hundred-dollar bill. "I need you to keep the Hennessy flowing. On the fifth refill, I want you to tell Gin, the lady doesn't want to see his glass empty."

"Gin don't have to pay for no drinks in here, lady," the waitress said.

"Yeah, I know, but I need you to let him know someone wanted to pay for him to drink tonight." The waitress eyed the bill again, then quickly snatched it from Nikki's hand.

"Okay, where you gonna be by the time he gets to the fifth drink?"

"Sitting directly across from him," Nikki said.

For the next hour, she watched from the darkest corner of the club as the waitress gave Gin refills on his drink. When she brought the fifth glass, Nikki saw her bend slightly to whisper in his ear. A few minutes later, she watched as Gin scanned the club.

When his gaze stopped at the bar, she smiled and held her glass up, as if she was making a toast.

Gin raised his glass, then motioned to one of the members in his entourage. He said something to the man, then swallowed his drink in one gulp.

"Nikki, Gin wants you at his table tonight," the voice came out of nowhere.

Nikki took her time and sashayed over to the table. She could see Gin acting as if he wasn't staring at her, but she knew she had him. *Finally,* she thought. They'd been working him for nearly two months.

Later that night, she sat in the passenger seat of Gin's Hummer as they zoomed down Westheimer.

"We not getting a room?" she asked as they drove in the opposite direction of the Hotel Derek.

"Later. Right now, I got a run I need to make. It's business, baby girl," he said. When they passed Highway 6, Gin turned to the right, and Nikki started wondering just where the hell they were going.

A black Blazer was waiting when Gin pulled up in the deserted park. Another truck pulled up and blocked Gin's Hummer. "Yo, stay put, I'll be back in a sec."

Nikki cracked her window, in hopes of hearing the conversation. She recognized the man from the bar as the one who got out of the truck and joined Gin as he walked up to two men. She heard Gin ask, "You got my shit?" She watched through the visor mirror as he looked quickly between the two men who stood in front of him.

"We wouldn't be here if we didn't," the shorter one said.

Gin looked them up and down again. "Y'all ain't five-o or nothin', right?"

"Man, I ain't got time for this shit!" the taller man yelled.

"Chill, man, chill," the short man warned.

"Bobby, we been doing business for a minute. The cash is all here, a cool quarter of a mil, you can count it if you need to." He smirked.

Gin nodded to his boy. "Get the cash, and give 'em their shit," he instructed.

The four men were near a deserted part of town; they were just behind George Bush Park in Houston. The road out there was deserted enough, at 3:00 A.M. After the deal went down, Gin watched his boy Sam climb into his truck and pull off, leaving Gin alone with his money and his treat: Nikki.

When Sam's taillights had long disappeared, Gin walked around to the passenger side of his Hummer. The only lights for miles came from his parking lamp, but it was enough for what he wanted to do. He glanced down inside the truck, but he didn't open the door. Instead, he walked to the back and opened the hatch to look at the two briefcases full of cash. Although he knew no one else was with them, he still looked around and saw darkness in every direction.

"C'mon out here, Nikki."

"Yes, boo," she cooed.

The door slowly opened and Nikki stepped out. By the time she arrived at the back of the Hummer, Gin had already used the cash to line the floor of the truck.

Nikki unzipped her bodysuit and stepped out of it. She was wearing a black lace thong and her pumps.

She tried to act indifferent to the mountain of cash laid out before her eyes.

She told herself she wasn't going to fuck tonight, but the sight of all that money made her coochie tingle, and it changed her mind. She instantly knew, she'd have to do whatever he might want; if that meant fucking, she'd be down. It was all business, and their motto was "Do whatever it takes to get the job done."

"Damn, Nikki. I wanna wax that ass right on top of all this paper." Gin smiled.

"And I want you to wax it too, baby." She smiled. "Just make sure you wax it real good," she cooed.

Gin extended his hand and helped her hop up into the truck.

"Damn, girl, that's what's up. You got enough room back there?"

Nikki stretched her body across the bills.

"That's right, baby girl. I like the look of that paper next to your skin, all over you. Yeah, that's what's up fo' real." He stroked his crotch.

"Why don't you come up here," Nikki said.

"Okay, but lemme see what I'm working with."

Nikki turned and got on all fours. With her ass in the air, she knew for sure she'd be fucking.

Gin reached for her ass. First he stroked it; then he rubbed his cheek next to it. "Damn, a nice phat ass. Girl, I can't wait to wax this." Gin took her hand and placed it on his stiff erection. "You ready for this, girl?"

"Bring it on. Let's do this," she said enthusiastically. "I been dreaming all night about you all up in me. Let's do this, baby."

Gin slipped off his pants and hopped up on the truck. With Nikki on her hands and knees, he eased his body behind her. He pulled his boxers down and rubbed his dick against her ass; first he stroked her cheek with his dick, then slipped it up the crack.

"Sssssss," Nikki moaned.

Gin reached forward and squeezed her breast. He pinched her nipple until she released a growling squeal. Then he reached his hand down to her clit and rubbed her wetness from the front to the back. Nikki closed her eyes tightly, anticipating his penetration.

He took the head of his dick and eased it into her asshole.

"C'mon, girl, you can take it. Ooooh, it's so nice and tight."

Nikki released the breath she had trapped in her throat. "Emm," she managed.

When he reached over and smacked her ass, she gyrated her hips and moved into his stiff erection.

"Nigga, if you know what's best for you, you'll stop right there!" a voice said.

"What the fuck!"

Nikki heard Gin scream. It felt as if his dick immediately lost its strength and quickly softened.

"Don't even think about reaching for no heat either. I'll blow your fucking brains out, right here."

"Aeey, man, we cool. Don't do nothing stupid," Gin said as he eased away from Nikki's inviting ass.

"What the hell is going on?" It was Nikki's turn to scream. There wasn't much light, but enough for her to see the shotgun aimed at her head. "Bitch, move slow. Hop your ass down and you might make it out alive."

"Oh, *ooo-kay.*" Nikki tried to hide her nervousness. She used her hands to cover up her bare breasts.

"It ain't even got to go down like this," Gin said.

Bam!

Bloop!

"Nigga, say another motherfuckin' word, and I'ma put some hot lead in your ass."

"Oh, my God, why'd you hit him?" Nikki screamed, and was about to move toward Gin, but the masked gunman poked her even harder with the barrel of his gun. While the two gunmen held Nikki and Gin at bay, a third man popped up with a duffel bag. In a quick, sweeping motion, he shoved all of the cash into the bag.

"I guess you could say you got caught slippin', huh?" a gunman teased.

Nikki sat quietly, waiting for the nightmare to be over. She and Gin had always talked about fucking on a bed of money—but, damn, she just wanted this shit to be over.

Before they left, the gunmen scooped up Nikki's and Gin's clothing, her purse, the cell phones, and the keys to his Hummer. Within minutes, the three took off on foot, and disappeared into the darkness of the night.

Regroup

Headquarters

Marleeta Brooks, in charge of the Headhunters, was manning the computer back in the suite at the Holiday Inn, at the airport. She was waiting to hear back from her crew. She tapped a key and once again checked their travel itinerary. Four of them were booked on an early flight first thing Tuesday morning. It was Sunday morning.

In the last briefing, she made it clear, they'd spend their last night in H-town together as a team, to make certain everyone made it back to LA together. While four would go by air, two would hit the road and drive back. In the last ninety days, the Headhunters had gone from Chicago to Houston. Now everybody was ready to get back to the left coast, and chill for a little while. That is, until the next project.

Just as she was about to retire for the night, she heard voices in the adjacent room. Marleeta looked up from the computer screen and focused on the connecting door. A few minutes later, there was a knock. "Queen Bee, you dressed?"

"Yeah who that?"

The door opened and Zack Cole stepped into her room.

"You guys are back already?"

"Yup, Trey and Danny Boy are unloading the truck. They coming," Zack said. A few minutes later, the other two men hauled in the large duffel bag. It was full and heavy.

"Damn, looks like we cleaned up, huh?" Marleeta got up from the desk and directed the men to pull the bag into the closet, next to the other three.

"'Nother day and we blowin' out, right? It's fuckin' hot in this bitch!" Zack said.

"Yeah, H-town ain't no joke," Marleeta said.

"Well, look, we 'bout to call it a night. We'll meet you downstairs for breakfast. You heard from Nikki or Tamara yet?" Danny Boy asked.

"Oh shit, we got something for Nikki." Trey ran back into their room and came back with Nikki's purse.

Marleeta's brow shot upward. "Damn, what you doin' with her bag?"

"We had to leave them stranded, so we couldn't just take his shit and leave hers," he said.

"Yeah, you got a point there. So I take it you guys didn't have any trouble tonight, huh?"

"Nope, nobody got shot," Zack said.

"Cool, that's what's up. I like it when shit goes smoothly. The way it's supposed to flow."

"Okay, look, I'll see you guys in the morning. Hopefully, the girls will be back by then and we can talk about what's next. Cool?"

"Cool," Zack said.

As soon as they closed the door, Marleeta pulled out a thick folder and started scanning through its pages. Usually, they only took the show on the road and tried to avoid doing shit close to home, but she'd been watching a few up-and-coming ballers.

She eased back on the queen-sized bed and flipped through the profile of one of the targets. "Oh yeah, he definitely ready. We could make this happen," she said.

Target: Jackson Donovan, aka JD
Holdings: a successful auto body shop, owns a fourplex building in Hollywood, a silent partner in several businesses, 2009 Hummer, two BMW SUVs
Estimated street net worth: 20 million
Drop schedule: the 15th & 1st monthly
Security detail: travels with entourage, made up of family members, two known addresses, moves around regularly
Weakness: a damsel in distress, struggling actresses, and singers
Misc: fetish for doggie style, loves to eat & work out

JD was a big hunk of a man. His hard body was tight with muscles spread over his powerful six-foot-three frame. Marleeta studied his pictures. She had decided long ago, she'd handle JD herself. Tamara had put in for him, when they briefly discussed him as a target, and Nikki said she wouldn't mind working him over, but the Queen Bee let it be known right away, JD was hers.

She caught heat just thinking about him, and how much fun she'd have with him. That same tingling sensation had returned to the spot between her legs. Each peek at his picture left her feeling hot and horny. Marleeta took her index finger and stuck it into her mouth. She held JD's picture in her left hand and slid her right into her panties.

She fingered her way around to her mound and started rubbing vigorously. Marleeta closed her eyes and pictured JD's strong arms spreading her legs. As her finger picked up momentum, she imagined his head being buried deep in her thighs. The faster her finger moved, the clearer his image became, the quicker his tongue flickered.

Marleeta could feel her heart beating faster. She released a wail and squeezed her eyes tighter. "Yes, JD, right there," she cried.

She dropped the picture and gripped the sheets with her left hand, all the while moving her index finger on her clit. She wanted that man, and she'd get him at all cost. As the sensation increased, she started panting. With her mind still on JD, she worked her clit, stroking and stroking. After a while, the tingling sensation rushed from the bottom of her feet, up her legs to her thighs, past her pulsating vagina, and through the rest of her body. Still clutching the sheet, she released a piercing scream, which brought Zack bursting through her door with his gun drawn.

"What the fuck!" he screamed.

"Damn, Zack, why you busting all up in my room and shit?" Marleeta hollered.

"Shit, I didn't know what was going on in here. I heard you screaming and shit. I thought somebody was up in here, up on you and shit."

"Nah, I'm just working some shit out," Marleeta said.

"Damn, Queen, you know all you had to do was

say the word and a brotha woulda broke you off. You ain't gots to handle that shit yourself." He smirked.

He grabbed his crotch at the sight of Marleeta's hand still between her legs.

"Boy, get your young ass outta here! I ain't trying to hold class up in here."

"Shit, you the one feelin' all on yourself. I may be young, but, shit, a nigga is packin'." He grabbed himself again.

"Pack your ass up outta here, and don't come barging into my room without knocking," she snarled.

"Yeah, well, keep it down while you up in here lovin' on yourself. Else a brotha gonna have to come in here and lay some pipe."

"Nigga, get your ass to bed."

Zack shook his head and closed the door. Marleeta got up and locked the door. She got back in bed and tried to go through JD's information again, but then decided against it. She had had enough excitement for one night. Besides, she thought, no use in wasting a good orgasm. Especially considering all the excitement it caused.

Background

Monday afternoon, Nikki came strolling into the hotel ten minutes after each other. Marleeta was just stepping out of the shower when she heard someone fumbling around in the sitting room. She peeked her head out of the bathroom door.

"Who's there?" she yelled.

"It's me, Queen Bee. You heard from Tamara yet?" Nikki responded.

"Naw, I'll be out in a sec."

Marleeta walked out, wrapped in a silk robe, and sat across from Nikki. She was wearing an old-school sweat suit, with matching blue tennis shoes.

"Girl, did Zack tell you they took my purse?"

"Yeah, he said they had to," Marleeta said.

"But, shit, I was like, 'How the hell am I gonna make it back?' That nigga Gin was on one for real, swearing he knew who them niggas was, and he was gonna kill them, they mamas, and they kids." Nikki shook her head. "He was all fucked up in the head. Said he wasn't tripping of the money, 'cause he'll make it back in a week, but, boy, that fool was hot."

"Who was?" Tamara asked as she walked into the room.

Marleeta looked at her. "Oh, she's talking about that nigga Gin, after the stickup."

"Oh, I'm sure he was hot. How much we get him for?" Tamara asked as she dropped her bag by the door.

"I don't know, but we made a killing. We need to haul ass out of town so we can rest, then get back on the grind," Marleeta answered.

Together, Marleeta, Nikki, and Tamara made up the Headhunters. Rumor had it, the group fucked for paper, ice, cars, and fine clothes. But that's only the image they portrayed. The truth was far more sinister. They traveled to large urban cities, knocking off niggas who were known for doing big things and flipping major paper. Home base for the crew was LA, but business kept them away from home quite often.

"Where are the boys?" Tamara asked.

"They probably still asleep," Marleeta answered, thinking about how Zack had busted in on her the night before.

"So me and Zack probably gonna drive back together. As soon as you guys get on the plane, we'll hop in the vehicle. If we drive straight through, we should be there by Wednesday afternoon," Marleeta said.

"I know you hate making that drive," Nikki said.

"Girl, please, with all that cheddar, that's the best road trip ever. I don't mind one bit," Marleeta said.

"So, Tamara, tell us how your set went down," Nikki encouraged.

"Well, it was all pretty smooth. I told you that GPS shit would make our gigs much easier. Leon was so extra careful, he had look-alikes that would drive out in every direction before he went in for the night."

"What? That nigga rollin' like that?" Nikki asked.

"Oh, he's large, that's for sure. I'll bet he halfway back to what we got him for already."

"You think we need to put him in the rotation again?" Marleeta asked.

Tamara shrugged and continued her story. "Anyway, he had some scrub pick me up. Girl, I had to wear a blindfold, and everything."

"Dang, he paranoid, huh?" Nikki chirped in.

"Well, when you rolling like that, I guess you can never be too careful," Tamara said.

"I know that's right," Marleeta said, getting up to slap high fives with her girls.

"So, anyway, we at the house. He ain't even want to go in the bedroom, and shit. We was about to get down right there in the living room—shit, I never even saw the rest of the house, but from what I could see, that nigga is living lovely." Tamara removed her coat.

"He had the nerve to have a fire blasting, and Cristal on ice. I kept thinking, 'Hmm, if this nigga wasn't about to get got, I might enjoy this.'" Tamara smiled. "So I'm doing my thang, you know, shaking up a little for a brotha, and he was like, 'Yeah, that's what I'm talking about.' I was like, 'It's all you, sweet Daddy.'" Tamara laughed.

"Not 'sweet Daddy,'" Marleeta teased.

"Girl, that shit be turning them dudes on like a motherfucka," Nikki said.

"So we, like, about to do that shit, then *bam*!" Tamara slapped her fist into the palm of her hand. "Them niggas bum-rushed the joint. But I'ma slap that nigga Danny Boy. He shoved that sawed-off to my chest a little harder than necessary."

"Well, you know he had to be convincing," Marleeta said.

"I know, but he really had a bitch scared, and shit. It's like he be in the zone. Sometimes I'm scared that little young fool might get trigger-happy. You know, like back in Philly, when the target pulled some heat, he was ready to blast on that fool."

"And he should have," Marleeta began. "Anytime those fools can't understand 'Don't move,' they oughta be shot."

"Yeah, but my ass ain't trying to die over no paper, I don't care how much we talking about," Nikki said.

Marleeta jumped up. "Well, you need to get the fuck out now, then, 'cause I'm serious about mine. And if you scared to take a fucking bullet, then you need to go get yourself a nine-to-five. If you gone be down with the Headhunters, you need to be down for whatever. You got that, Nikki?"

"Damn, Queen, why you all up in my face, and shit? You know I'm straight."

Marleeta glared at Nikki, then at Tamara. "This is our livelihood, I got to know when you guys are out there, you working it with all you got. So if them niggas put a gun to your fucking head, then you just do what the fuck they ask. Act like your ass really scared for your life. Think about what would happen if any of those fools ever got a clue about our hustle. Shit, we wouldn't be able to lay our heads down proper."

"Yeah, I feel you," Nikki said. She watched as Marleeta sat back down.

"Now, what happened after they left with the

money?" she asked, starting to lather lotion on her legs.

"Shit, he started walking around, organizing his crew, trying to get a line on who set him up. After about three hours of him working the phones, he looked over at me. I hadn't said anything. I was just sitting there, looking pissed and scared." Tamara shook her head. "You know that fool didn't even let me go into the bathroom to shower. He told me I could wash up in the guest bathroom. When he tried to make me put the blindfold back on to leave, I told him he was crazy. I was like, 'If you think you gotta worry about me coming back out here, you must be crazy.' I was like, 'I don't need this shit. You cool and all, but I'm heading back down to North Carolina.'"

"That's right, you told that nigga you was from North Carolina. Didn't he think it was odd you don't talk with a twang?"

"Let's just say he ain't the sharpest knife in the drawer. He a helluva hustler, though, 'cause that house was laid. Anyway, after we fought about the blindfold, he drove me back to the apartments. He didn't even wait to see me walk through the gates. That nigga swore he was gonna bring it to them fools. That's all he kept talking about. I'd hate to be them niggas whoever they are," Tamara said.

"So he dropped you at the apartments. You heard back from him yet?"

Tamara shook her head. "I don't think I have to worry about him. That fool is twisted. He got real tunnel vision. He wants to see blood for what happened to him."

"Well, we'll be long gone if he ever makes the connection," Marleeta assured.

"Oh, I handled mines, he ain't gonna connect that shit to me. Because we had the GPS working, Zack and them didn't even have to follow me. They simply waited about an hour and drove right up to the house like they were invited. That shit was sweet, if I have to say so myself."

Marleeta, satisfied that her body would be soft and moisturized, got up and walked toward the bedroom. "I told the boys I'd take them out to eat before we get up outta here," she said over her shoulder.

The moment her door closed, Nikki slid next to Tamara. "You see how she flashed on me?" she whispered. "She been tripping out like that a lot lately. I'm telling you, it's gonna be Dallas all over again."

Tamara looked toward the bedroom door. She didn't want any part of Nikki's foolishness. She was happy being part of the Headhunters, but for the last six months or so, Nikki had been trying to convince her that they should branch out and do their own thing.

"Girl, Dallas was a fluke. Queen is straight. She said she going straight to the top, and she's taking us right along with her. I don't know about you, but I like my lifestyle. We ain't got the connections Queen got. We don't see all the behind-the-scene shit she got to do to prep our targets."

Nikki sucked her teeth. "Why you scared, and shit? Imagine what we could do if we were running things. That new Jag you want, girl, you'd probably be rolling that, and then some." Nikki shook her head. "I don't know how much longer I can deal with her mood swings and attitude coming up outta nowhere—that's all I'm saying."

Tamara stood. "Well, all I'm saying is I like this little setup we got, and I like it just the way it is. I ain't going nowhere. Queen gives us the target, the information we need, we handle the rest, and we all get paid." Tamara shrugged. "What could be better than that?"

Nikki rolled her eyes and sucked her teeth again. She got up and walked into the room she shared with Tamara.

Marleeta sat on the side of the bed, facing the wall. She was furious. It was the second time Nikki had challenged her, and she was growing tired of the confrontation. She promised herself, one more time, and she'd have to find a replacement. The truth was, she knew she needed each of her crew members. But she often wondered why the women couldn't be as easy as the guys. The guys—give them their cut, take them out every once in a while, and they're happy. It was that simple. The women, on the other hand, always posed a different challenge. If things went smoothly, they'd be able to retire in two more years. And Marleeta had big plans. She was taking her money and moving to Belize.

There the U.S. dollar was double its value, which meant $500,000 would be a smooth million. Marleeta wasn't flashy, she lived well, but she didn't overdo it. One million would be more than enough for her to live on. But she also knew if she stayed in the game for another two years, she might be able to get away with at least $2 million U.S.—a sweet stash, and more than enough to help her make a clean getaway.

She was planning an exploratory trip, once they made it back to LA. Her goal was to take some money down there and start building her dream house. Marleeta had love for the States, but she saw how hard black and brown people had it, and was determined not to have to waste away her most productive years punching a time clock.

It hadn't always been that way. Marleeta spent most of her life with her grandmother. No depressing drug-addict story or jailhouse blues. Marleeta's mother was a hardworking single mother. She spent so much time at work, Marleeta's grandmother was left to raise her. Marion Brooks worked for the San Bernardino Police Department. After earning her bachelor's degree in criminal justice, she moved up the ranks. And while she hoped she was setting a good example for her only daughter, that example showed Marleeta working hard could be rewarding, but it could also be deadly.

One night, Marion was working the overnight shift for another officer, whose maternity leave was extended. During a break, Marion walked into the women's locker room. At six in the morning, when the next shift arrived for work, her body was found in one of the bathroom stalls. Marleeta would later learn her mother suffered from an aneurysm. No one knew for sure how long she had lain on the bathroom floor, dying. Marleeta, however, was convinced the job—its taxing hours, the constant drive to be recognized for her dedication—was what really killed her mother.

Marion Brooks had been Marlene Johnson's pride

and joy. When her husband died, she lived for her only child, working hard to fulfill her husband's last wishes—that his daughter receive a college education. When Marleeta's grandmother Marlene suffered a mild stroke, she secretly hoped it would serve as a warning to her own mother.

But Marion continued to work, stress, and push the envelope. Two years after her own mother's death, Marleeta closed the casket on her grandmother, her only living relative. She never knew her father, but she never felt unloved or alone *until* she lost both her mother and grandmother. She took the insurance money from her mother's policy and put that in the bank. Two years later, she used the money from her grandmother's policy and did the same.

Marleeta stayed in an emotional funk for months after her grandmother died. With the house paid for, she had to figure out what she'd do with the rest of her life. She had no desire to go to college, but she knew her ninety-thousand dollars wouldn't last forever. The moment she decided to treat herself to a complete makeover might have changed the course her life was set to take. She had to venture into South Central Los Angeles for a hair appointment. As she made her way out of the famous cuttin' up, she bumped into the man of her dreams. Stoney was his name, and he was fly, bigger than life itself.

It took no time for them to become inseparable. Wherever you saw Stoney, Marleeta was soon to follow. Stoney made money faster than either of them could handle, and he was coming up at record speed. It didn't take long for others to notice the ghetto star that was quickly on the rise, and the sexy female who stayed glued to his side.

So when a young hustler wanted to make his mark on the streets, he figured he'd hit Stoney where it counts to send a message. One night as Marleeta left the hair shop and walked to her car, parked in the back, she felt a cold metal barrel pointed to the back of her head.

"You take us to Stoney and we might not kill you," the cold voice said.

She was shaking so much, she didn't know quite what to do.

"I don't know where he at," she had cried.

Smack!

"That's for the lie," he said.

Marleeta could feel the bump developing on the back of her head. Tears started racing down her cheeks. *"Ohh, oo-kay,"* she cried.

She felt like a low-life snake leading the masked gunman to her man's hideout, but what choice did she have? As they piled into her car and made her drive, with the gun still on her, she kept thinking of ways she could send a warning out to Stoney. But there was nothing she could do. She kept hoping someone would see the fools in her car, but her windows had a dark tint. They drove and pulled up at the house on Third Avenue, off Crenshaw. Still, she wondered if she should yell and try to warn Stoney, but the opportunity never presented itself.

At the door, the gunmen motioned for her to pull out her key to unlock the door. She did. A few minutes later, she walked in and heard the shower running.

"That you, babe?"

Two gunmen ran toward the sound of the shower, and one stayed with her.

"Babe, I'm sorry!" Marleeta screamed, but it was too late. When she tried to run, the gunman tackled her and they tumbled to the floor. Marleeta scratched at his eyes and ripped his shirt. The last thing she saw was a multicolored tattoo of a scorpion on his chest.

Smack! Bam! Bam!

Marleeta had passed out. She later learned the gunman robbed Stoney, shot him, and left when they thought both of them were dead. She was struck with the gun twice, once they tumbled to the floor.

Despite her struggles, she couldn't get thoughts of that day out of her mind. She was riddled with what-ifs—what if she would've led them to the wrong house? What if Stoney hadn't been at home? What if she hadn't insisted Stoney move his gun out of the bathroom and he would've been able to come out blasting?

To clear her head and get away, she joined her only friend on a trip to Belize. It was there, she decided she'd move and retire in the small country. Marleeta's life had been filled with so much death and destruction, she wasn't sure she'd be able to go on. But she did. And every time she thought about her retirement plans, she became more determined to come up with a hustle to help stack the cash she needed.

To this day, she never found out who had killed Stoney. But in her dreams, she felt like she'd one day face the man who had changed the course her life was set to take. In the meantime, she decided to be on the other side of the stickup, cleaning niggas out for all they got. That was nearly three years ago.

She'd been going strong ever since. It wasn't hard to recruit the rest of the team.

Tamara had the reputation as a fierce gold digger. She didn't have any qualms about fucking for money. And she loved the finer things in life. Marleeta and Tamara had known Nikki from around the way. It was Tamara who pulled in her two younger cousins, Zack and Danny. They brought dog Trey on the road, and the crew had been working together ever since.

Zack and Danny were the big guns. They both stood a beefy six feet three inches tall, and weighed in at around 235 pounds. They were only eighteen when they started with the Headhunters. Trey was nineteen.

The knock on the connecting door jarred her out of those sad thoughts from the past.

"Yo, Queen Bee, whassup? We going to eat or what?" Zack asked through the door.

"Yeah, see if Nikki and Tamara are coming," Marleeta yelled back.

"Cool, we're going down to the lobby. Hurry," Zack screamed.

Marleeta was last to leave the room. She hung the sign on the doorknob, indicating she did not want the cleaning service, and walked to the elevator.

Homecourt

By the time Marleeta and Zack pulled into her driveway off Central and 124th, they were both worn-out. It was more than the thirty-four-hour drive from Houston to LA that had her spent, it was the combination of that, along with the nagging conversation with Zack about why he couldn't hit it.

"I don't fuck with young boys," she told him.

"You shouldn't knock it till you try it," he countered. "This young buck will have you climbing the walls, pulling out your hair, and shit," he promised.

"Yeah, but I don't get down like that, so we'll never get to find out, huh?"

"See, Queen, a woman like you need a young strapping brotha like me. Shit, girl, you could train me to do all the freaky shit you like. Don't think I don't know what you be doing to yourself all locked up in those rooms, all alone and shit."

"Oh yeah, what's that?"

He shot her a look. "C'mon, Queen, I may be

young in age, but a nigga like me got mad skills and experience."

She laughed.

"For real, though. I ain't lying. I can lay some pipe. I ain't even bullshitting you. And, shit, I know how to eat some pussy too."

Marleeta laughed at that confession. "Boy, what you know about eating pussy?" She chuckled.

"I know how to use my tongue to light that shit up. Believe that. See them old heads, they too busy trying to slop the lips, but that ain't even my style."

"Oh, is that so?" Marleeta asked.

"Yeah, peep this. First I stroke the cat, real softlike, with the very tips of my fingers. I use my fingertips to spread the lips open, you know, that way I can go straight to the clit. Then I take my tongue, but first I swallow my spit, though, 'cause I don't need to be spitting all up in the pussy. If I do what I'm supposeta, the pussy gonna be overflowing with wetness soon enough. So I take my tongue, and I place it right on top of the clit. I just sit there for a few seconds, so you can feel the heat and soft pressure from my tongue. But, see, I'm tasting you all the while." He glanced off the road and over at Marleeta.

"So, while my tongue is just resting on the clit, I start to slowly move it up and down, you know, just to create a little friction, but not too much at first. I just let my tongue glide up and down that clit—then I press it a little harder."

"So when do you put your fingers in?" Marleeta asked, egging him on.

"Nah, see, that's what I'm talking about. I ain't into using my fingers to fuck you. I told you, I'm hung, so that's what I got this big-ass dick for. My fingers are only there to aid in my mission to separate the clit from its hiding place. Now I'm not talking about sucking your clit—there's a big difference, trust me. I got my tongue rubbing up against your clit, and that's all I do, just rub up and down, up and down. See, the trick is to keep rubbing without moving away from the clit. It ain't as easy as it sounds. It takes a real soldier to get up in there and massage the clit like that. I always keep contact with the clit, that's the real key." He tapped the steering wheel. "See, all along, I'm rubbing and killing you softly."

As he spoke, Marleeta hung on his every word. She could just about feel what he was describing if she closed her eyes, but she refused to do that. No way in hell was she gonna let this little young nigga know he was starting to get to her. Shit, she never knew there were different ways to eat the coochie. She figured a man went down there, fingered a few times, slopped, sucked, licked, and then she came. But let this young nigga tell it, there was actually an art to eating pussy. And his ass had the nerve to sound like he really knew what he was talking about too. The nerve, she thought.

"So, by the time I back off, that cat is so wet, I literally slip in and out. And I'm packing too, so that's saying a lot." He hit his chest. "I mean, look at me. I've been this size since I was, like, fourteen. I ain't never known what it was like to have a little boy's dick. I'm hung for real." He shrugged. "Hmm, I must get that shit from my pops, 'cause he walked out on us when I was a baby, but to this day my moms still sings his praises. That just tells me, he was working with something major. And you know they say, the apple don't fall far from the tree."

"You know what else they say, Zack." Marleeta decided to fuck with his head a bit.

"Nah, what's that?" he asked.

"Well, they say, those who brag about what they got ain't really packing at all."

In one quick move, Zack removed his right hand from the steering wheel, grabbed Marleeta's left hand from the CD player, and put it at his crotch.

"Damn." She quickly pulled her hand back.

"Yeah, boy! See, that's what I'm talking about. And he ain't even all the way woke either. So you could just imagine what I'm working with, girl. I'm telling you, I'm hung. I'm like a triple threat. I'm a pussy connoisseur, I'm hung, and I'm an all-nighter! *Shiiiit,* beyoches be stressing me hard. I'm for real, though."

Marleeta's mind was really racing. She couldn't believe what she felt when he led her hand to his crotch. His worm felt thick, and she immediately got wet. If he wasn't so young, she'd demand that they pull over, right on the side of Interstate 10 and take care of business. She had no idea Zack was packing like that.

"Hmm, why you quiet all of a sudden, huh? I done put something on your mind, huh?"

Marleeta released a nervous giggle. "Boy, I ain't thinking 'bout your young ass. You just better drive this truck so we can make good time." She pressed a button that allowed her seat to recline all the way back, and closed her eyes.

"Oh, so you 'bout to go to sleep on a nigga now? Whassup with that?" He looked at her. "Queen, here you want to reach out and feel something you could dream about?"

"Boy, leave me alone." She turned her head toward the window and tried not to think about why this young-ass boy was packing more than most men she had been with so far.

Hours later, when he woke her up and told her they had finally made it home, Marleeta had been having a wet dream. She was being fucked, froggy-style, by a man with a dick the same size she imagined Zack's was.

Marleeta slept the entire day, Thursday. She had called a meeting for Friday evening, and Tamara was the first to arrive. She walked in with a bag of food.

"I don't know if you ate yet, but I brought Roscoe's for the meeting," she said as she passed Marleeta.

"Cool, I was just wondering what to order," Marleeta said as she let Tamara in.

"Damn, girl, it's dark in here."

"Shit, I've been trying to catch up on sleep after that marathon car ride. Your cousin is a straight fool. With his young ass," Marleeta said.

"Girl, you betta watch him. I don't know what he be doing, but my auntie says those young girls be staking out her place looking for him. She said she gets no rest when he's gone on business, they be straight fiending."

"Hmm, wonder what that's all about?" Marleeta said, remembering their time on the road.

"I don't know, but them young girls act like he got the magic stick or something. They be straight losing their minds over that little nigga."

Before Marleeta could say another word, the door-bell rang. "You want me to get that?" Tamara asked.

"Yeah. It's probably Nikki."

When Tamara walked back in, Nikki was at her side. "Queenie, I brought some Hypnotiq." She smiled.

"Well, bust that shit open," Marleeta said. "I hope it's the big bottle too. You know that little shit is only good for three glasses, and I don't know about you guys, but I ain't trying to be teased."

"For real," Tamara said.

"Okay, here's the split from Leon in Houston. There are one hundred ten Gs for each of you. Fifty Gs for the boys, and I'm at one-thirty. Is that cool?" Marleeta asked. She pulled out a calculator and started punching numbers. "Okay, that was the first job in H-town. From Gin, we each clear a little over twenty-five Gs, the boys get ten each. We straight?"

"Hell yeah," Tamara screamed. "When's our next gig? A bitch like me trying to build a serious bankroll, if you know what I mean."

"Yeah, I feel you," Marleeta said.

Nikki sat quietly counting her money.

"Okay, we should lay low for the next few weeks. You know, party it up a little, nothing too big. Maybe we could go out to the Valley and see what's shaking there. Then next month, I got Denver lined up. That's for you, Tamara. I'm still working on a target for Nikki. By the time we're ready to roll, I'll have it all worked out," Marleeta proposed.

"What about JD?" Nikki asked.

"What about him?" Marleeta wanted to know.

"When we gonna hit that. I heard he's building some apartments on the east side. We need to strike before that nigga changes zip codes on our asses and we miss out altogether."

"Yeah, I'm working on JD."

"Shit, Queen, you been saying that shit for months now. Whassup with you when it comes to JD? It's like you keep putting him off. Is there something we should know?"

Marleeta tried to hush Nikki with a glaring stare, but Nikki was far gone.

"Shit, from what I hear, he doing big thangs out there. I say we need to reel him in before he gets beyond our reach. What you think, Tamara?" Nikki completely ignored the look Marleeta was sending her way.

Tamara looked between the two. "I just hope he don't stop hugging those corners by the time we ready to move. I could imagine it would be harder for us to track him down."

"JD ain't going nowhere," Marleeta insisted.

"How you know?" Nikki challenged. "A lot of niggas talking about getting out of the game. Shit, for all we know, he could be one of 'em."

"Let me handle JD, Nikki. That's the way we do things, right? I got this under control."

"Hmm, well, I can't tell," Nikki mumbled.

"What did you say?" Marleeta asked.

Tamara quickly spoke up. "When are the boys coming through? You want me to take them their money?" she asked.

For a few minutes, no one said a word. Nikki continued counting her money, like she didn't hear

Marleeta, and Tamara was hoping they'd be able to avoid a huge fight.

"Naw, we straight. Zack called right before you came. He said they'll shoot through in a couple of hours. I wanted us to meet before they got here anyway. I say we chill for the next few days. You know, let me get a handle on a few things and see about something in the Valley."

Marleeta looked at Nikki and Tamara. Nikki was still counting her money. Tamara had started eating. "Tamara, you've been talking about a cruise. Why don't you try to catch one of those three-day specials. Grab one of your boy toys and go have some fun."

Tamara shrugged. "I don't know. But a few days off wouldn't hurt. What are you gonna do, Nikki?"

"I got plans. I could use a week off. Shit, we all can." She glanced at Marleeta for a split second. "Why don't you tell us what you're planning on doing," she said.

Marleeta glared at her. "I'll think of something," she said. "But right now, I'm concerned about you guys. I don't want anybody to get burned out."

Nikki kissed a wad of cash. "Baby, as long as we keep stacking paper like this, you ain't got to worry about me getting bored, or burned, or whatever the hell you worrying about."

The doorbell rang, and Tamara jumped up to get it.

"Hey! It's payday around this beyoch!" Trey yelled as he followed in, behind Zack and Danny Boy. When they walked into the dining room, where Nikki and Marleeta sat, they started swapping high fives.

"We closing out another successful work session?" Zack asked no one in particular.

"Yup." Marleeta passed an extra large padded envelope to Danny Boy, Zack, then Trey. Each had *$60G* written in small letters on the outside.

Danny Boy's eyes lit up. "Damn! Sixty Gs, that's what's up. That's what the fuck I'm talking about. A nigga like me 'bout to set it off. I'ma go buy me some pussy, liquor, and a real good time."

Trey elbowed Danny Boy and everyone in the room chuckled. "Damn fool, whassup?"

"Okay, everybody's been paid. Now, don't spend it all in one place," Marleeta warned. Twenty minutes later, everyone had left, except Zack, who said he needed to holla at Marleeta for a minute.

Just Got Paid . . .

Nikki couldn't leave Marleeta's house fast enough. Her tires peeled as she burned rubber turning the block. She was headed straight to the Normandie Casino, and if luck was on her side, she could double, maybe even triple, her money in a matter of hours. She felt lucky too.

As she drove, Nikki thought about Marleeta, calling herself "Queen Bee." *What kind of shit is that*? In the beginning, when they first hooked up, it was all gravy. Queenie didn't have the big head she walked around with most days. Back then, they all agreed on a target before making a move. Then there was a rotation, none of this "off-limits" shit. Now, all of a sudden, Queenie wanted to dictate who they could mark and when. Shit, she just wanted to keep JD all to herself.

Well, Nikki decided, after her fun at the casino, she'd try again to talk Tamara into venturing out. The way she saw it, all they had to do was make a few jobs on the side, and Queenie never even had to know. She'd get Zack and maybe Danny Boy—the four of 'em, they could probably pull it off. She was confident they could.

Nikki swung her Range Rover into the Normandie's full parking lot. She grabbed her large Louis Vuitton duffel and dumped her cash into it. She glanced around the parking lot in both directions, then slammed her trunk shut. Nikki was so excited she could hardly walk straight and steady as she rushed toward the lobby.

"Nikki, how good to see you," the security guard said.

"Aey, Bob, I know it's been a minute, but I'm feeling lucky today."

"Well, I hope you're right." He smiled. "I'm sure this is your day. Your lucky day," he said as he held the door open for her.

Nikki looked around the first-floor room. She noticed familiar faces at the blackjack table and even a few at the slots. A barmaid passed. "Hey, Nikki, where you been, girl?"

"Oh, here and there," she said.

"A Panty Ripper?" the waitress asked.

"You know it."

"I'll meet you at the blackjack table in the high roller's room, right?"

"Girl, you know me too well," Nikki said as she walked to the back, where stakes started at $5,000. When Nikki pulled up at her normal spot, the dealer winked at her.

"Jeffery," she said as he shuffled.

Three hours later, Nikki was up fifty grand. A small crowd had formed around her and she felt great. Something had told her this would be her lucky day, and she was right. With a Panty Ripper in one hand, and her fingers from the free hand flipping through her chips, she felt on top of the world.

"Damn, how you feelin', Nikki?" a voice asked.

"Just got paid, so you know I'm living real large." She giggled.

At the rate she was going, Nikki had no doubt she'd be able to double her loot before sun up. She was used to brining up the sun inside the Normandie, and she had no problem doing it again. After all, she was on a mission and she had finally reclaimed her lucky streak. That streak had avoided her for months.

After losing big nearly two years ago, she had stumbled out of the Normandie, depressed, broke, and desperate.

As luck would have it, she bumped into Marleeta and Tamara at a nearby IHOP.

Nikki had just let $25,000 slip through her fingers after pulling an all-nighter inside the Normandie. She escaped with $20 in her pocket, and she decided she'd go to IHOP to try and figure out how she could possibly get at least half her money back.

As she was being led to a table in the back, she passed Tamara and Marleeta huddled in a booth.

Tamara looked up at her and smiled. "Nikki, girl, is that you?"

Caught a bit off guard, Nikki snapped out of her stupor and remembered her old classmate Tamara. "Yeah, girl, damn. I ain't seen you in more than a minute. What's crackin'?"

"Same ole, same ole," Tamara said. "Hey, this is my new business partner, Marleeta. Marleeta, Nikki."

"Business partner?" Nikki asked. She noticed how good Marleeta and Tamara looked. Nothing too extravagant, subtle things, like the large diamond studs in Marleeta's ears, or the designer bags they both had by their sides.

Nikki wasn't sure what kind of business the two were in, but she knew she wanted to be a part of whatever they had going on.

That day, after being up all night and losing every red cent she had, Nikki listened as Tamara and Marleeta told her how they made money. She was eager to get in, couldn't wait to bait a nigga, and take him for all his money.

But sixty days after they had agreed to bring her on, Marleeta still hadn't allowed Nikki to pull a target of her own. She sat back and watched as the two women transformed themselves into exactly what the target liked, right before her eyes. If it meant wigs, a change of hair color, titties taped down, or certain clothes to accentuate specific body parts, whatever the target liked, they became it—they fit the mold, then went to work.

Sometimes they would prep a target for weeks, even months before making a move. And when they struck, everything was carefully calculated. Nikki knew one thing for sure—Marleeta, who did most of the legwork, was serious about her paper, and they worked hard to rake it in.

After the first payoff, Nikki nearly choked when the take was more than fifty grand! Then, when Marleeta let her hold ten grand for just sitting through training, she thought she had died and gone straight to heaven. Despite the fact that she lost every penny of that ten grand at the casino, she remembered holding that money in the palm of her hands. The ten grand didn't even look like a whole lot of cash, the way she imagined it would. It was like a neat stack of one-hundred-dollar bills with a rubber band around it.

By the time it was her turn, Nikki was hungry. She nearly messed up by fucking her target, Trigger, before they made it back to the location where he kept his stash. It was a good thing he was a sex fiend, because she had no idea how she would've explained that one. But Trigger had the nerve to be sexy as hell, and every fifteen minutes he had to remind her how much he loved a big phat ass like hers. That shit turned her the fuck on instantly.

She was supposed to wait, try to draw out foreplay for as long as possible—but, shit, he kept whispering sweet things in her ear, started sucking on her neck in that spot, and pinched her nipples. She rode his ass raw right there in the front seat.

In order to get him back to the house, she had to promise him some out-of-this-world head. Nikki was so glad when Danny Boy and his crew kicked in the door. Her jaws were tired and that fool was nowhere near coming. Nikki had to remind herself to act scared and surprised by the attack, but, honestly, she felt like she was being rescued.

The cheers that erupted from her small fan club brought her back to the blackjack table, where she was now up $75,000. *Sweet.* She heard someone behind her whisper, "I'd take my money and go home."

But Nikki had other plans. Her hand was itching and she knew for sure her time had come. She raised the stake and sat back to glow in what was clearly her moment.

Tamara had her cousin Danny Boy drop her off at home. She was tired of trying to ward off battles between Queen Bee and Nikki. But damn—she did love paydays. Tamara didn't feel the slight bit of guilt about robbing these ballers. They had more than enough money to spare, and she didn't mind help-ing relieve them of some of it.

With the money she had made working, she bought herself a little house in Carson. Tamara felt good when she was able to spend time at home. Her house was already paid off. She bought the small two-bedroom with cash, and had it in her mother's name. They soon added her to the deed as co-owner, and she'd been living there for nearly two years.

Tamara also used her money to help pay off the mortgage on her mother's house. When her mother asked where she had gotten all of that money, she lied and said she got a job as an extra in a low-budget movie that had done well in Europe.

Tamara walked into her small walk-in closet and moved the wooden dresser to the side. She started fiddling with the combination to the safe she had installed. Most of her money went inside that safe. She would occasionally deposit just under nine thousand in cash to bank accounts, and often she spread some money to her safe-deposit box she had bought at the bank.

She knew of Marleeta's plans to retire in a few years, and she didn't want to be left out in the rain. Every once in a while, Tamara would splurge on an expensive piece of jewelry or a designer label, but she didn't like to do that too often, because she felt like it made Marleeta nervous.

Marleeta had always warned that they shouldn't go overboard to attract any unwanted attention. And Tamara had listened and learned well. Lately she had started thinking about what she might want to do when the cash flow dried up. As she was putting the cash into the safe, her phone rang.

Tamara stuffed the money inside and slammed the steel door shut. She turned the knob on the door and slid the dresser back in place. She caught the phone just before the machine clicked on.

"Hello?"

"Damn, baby, you real hard to catch. I started thinking maybe you gave a brotha the wrong number or something."

At first, Tamara was silent, hoping the caller would keep talking so she could try and catch the voice.

"You don't know who this is, huh?"

"I confess, I don't. You got me," she said.

"This Mark, boo."

"Mark. Damn! Hey, how you doing?" she asked. Their last tryst suddenly popped into her head. She wouldn't mind going at it again with Mark, but she'd be damned if she'd ask.

"So whassup, lady? I swear, I never thought I'd get you on the phone again."

"I travel a lot," she said.

"Yeah, you a flight attendant, right?"

Tamara didn't remember telling him that, but if that's what he thought, she wasn't gonna go trying to explain that she jacked men for a living. "I stay gone, and they know how to work a sistah too."

"Well, are you off for a couple of days?"

"Yup!"

"Looking for something to get into?"

"You know it." She beamed.

"Why don't we go out to the Marina. We could grab dinner, and see where it goes from there."

"How about you give me two hours. I just walked in. I need to run a couple of errands, but I could meet you at your place. You still got that spot near the Fox Hills Mall?" Tamara asked.

"Cool, you remember," Mark said.

Tamara sat across the table from Mark at an out-side table in El Torito, on the Marina. As he made small talk, her mind kept thinking about how she could initiate sex without coming across too obvious.

"So what are you doing after dinner?" Tamara asked.

"No plans. You can have me all night, if you want. Wanna see a movie, stroll the boardwalk, or whatever you in the mood for," he said.

"All night, huh?"

"All night. And I won't bite, unless that's what you want," he teased.

Tamara sipped her margarita and thought about being with Mark again. Here she was, sitting on a grip of cash, and about to get her freak on. Life couldn't be any better.

"I have an idea," she began. "We've both been drinking a lot. I don't think we should drive, so maybe we should walk over to the Sheraton and get a room. That way, we could drink some more, and see what happens. How does that sound?"

"Waiter, check, please," Mark yelled, with his hand in the air.

After checking into their room, Mark and Tamara strolled into the hotel's bar. They ordered another round of margaritas, and were halfway through when Tamara summoned the bartender. "Would we be able to order a pitcher of margaritas through room service?"

"I think we'd be able to accommodate that request. Give me your room number and I'll have it sent right up."

Tamara paid their tab, left the waiter a nice tip, and nearly dragged Mark up to the room. If memory served her correctly, she knew she was in for a treat. Inside the room, they could hardly wait for the pitcher of margaritas to be brought up. Tamara had stripped down to her matching bra and panty set, and was fucking Mark with her eyes.

"Damn, you look even better than I remember," he said.

Tamara sat across from him in the wing chair and spread her legs. "I take it, you like what you see," she teased.

"Huh, you just don't know, girl!" he said.

By the time the pitcher arrived, Mark was more than ready to get busy. He quickly went to the door.

He took the pitcher and tossed some cash at the bellhop. "Thanks!" He slammed the door shut and stripped down to his boxers and wife beater.

When he walked over to Tamara to refill her empty glass, he nearly dropped the entire pitcher. With her panties tossed to the side on the floor, she used her finger to rub the lips of her visibly wet pussy.

"Damn, girl, you ready, huh?" He poured a drink for himself, then took his seat across from her. "Shit, the view is excellent from here," he said.

"You like this?"

"Oh, fuck yeah. I like it a lot." He sipped his drink.

Tamara took one breast into her hand and stretched it up to her lips. She used her tongue to circle her nipple, then held it between her teeth. After a few minutes, she went back to her pussy, now fingering herself slowly.

Mark watched her every move. "I wonder what that tastes like with some margarita on it," he said.

"There's only one way to find out for sure," she said.

Mark took his glass and held it close to her crotch. He carefully angled it to the side, allowing a little to drip down into her pussy.

"*Oooooh shit.* That's cold. But I like it." She smiled.

"Then you'll like this even better," Mark said as he bent down and sopped up the liquid from her lips and lingered at her clit. There he sucked, until he was certain her mound was dry. Satisfied that it was, he leaned back to examine his work. Again he tilted his glass just so, watched as Tamara cringed from the icy sensation, then dipped his head to suck up the drink.

After he finished, Tamara had come three times

and was all but begging him to flip her over the arm of the chair and fuck her from behind.

Mark was all too happy to do exactly as he was told. His dick wasn't huge, but she felt him as he entered her. She immediately sucked him in deeper.

"Shit, Tamara, your fine ass got some good pussy," he cried out.

"Fuck it like you mean that then," Tamara taunted.

And he did. They fucked over the back of the wing chair, then moved to the coffee table, and if that wasn't enough, he lifted her up from the table, held her ass in his hands, and slammed her back up against the wall.

"How you like it? How does it feel?"

"Oh, you hitting my spot, Mark. You hitting my spot," she purred.

"Gooo-ood. Thha-t's whaaa-t I'm here to do. Hit your sppp-ot!"

"*Yeeesssss,* that's it. Right there. That's it, Mark, right there!" She screamed.

"Where? Right there?"

"Yes, baaa-by. Ohhh *yessssss*!"

Mark bent his knees, grabbed her hips tighter, and dug deeper into her.

Sweating and panting now, Tamara couldn't believe she was about to come for the fourth time in a single night. She and Mark had been fucking for nearly two hours!

"You say that you want it. . . . You say that you need it. Is it gooood for you?"

"Oh, fuck yes! Yes! Yes! *Yeeesss!* Please don't stop! Don't you dare stop! You're hitting my spot, Mark!"

They were nearly startled into stopping when they

heard banging on the wall. That only encouraged Mark to take her to the bed. Before he had the chance to lay her on her back, she flipped him over and mounted him.

Tamara stretched her back to his knees, then rotated her hips in a slow and seductive grind. With his dick still inside her going strong, she slowed her rotation and moved her hips in circular motions.

All Mark could do was throw his head back and release a menacing grunt from the pit of his belly. Tamara used the muscles in her pussy to clutch his hard dick. With a tight grip on his member, she eased up, with her hands cupping her breasts.

Mark opened his eyes and caught a glimpse of her squeezing her nipples, and he started moving his hips faster to match her pace. Tamara leaned forward and allowed her breasts to hang into his face.

"Suck 'em," she begged.

He grabbed her breasts, squeezed them together, and slopped each nipple, before he took one between his teeth. This drove her insane. She grabbed his chest with her nails and dug into his flesh.

"Please don't stop. I'm almost there," she huffed.

"I'm with you, girl, I'm with you. You like this, huh?"

"Oh yes! *Yeesss!*" Tamara cried. "Right there! I'm—I'm—I'm commming!" she screamed.

"It's about fuckin' time!" a voice yelled through the walls.

But Mark and Tamara were both in the zone. He exploded the second he felt her juices overflowing. They collapsed next to each other, struggling to breathe.

"Damn, girl, that's some bomb-ass pussy you got there," Mark said.

"And you knew exactly what to do with it," she huffed.

Marleeta was glad Nikki had left as quickly as she had. Marleeta didn't want to alarm the others, but she was beginning to think Nikki had some serious issues. She was also hoping those issues wouldn't affect business.

After walking Danny Boy, Trey, and Tamara to the door, she wished Zack would've left too. However, he sat posted on her leather sofa, like he owned the place. When he picked up the remote and started flipping through the channels, she nearly started panicking. How in the hell would she get rid of this little boy?

She watched him from the foyer. He looked comfortable, childlike even, as he sat giggling at something on TV. Marleeta shook her head. She felt uncomfortable in her own damn house.

"Yo, Queen, you wanna go grab some food, a drink or something?" he asked, eyes still glued to the tube.

"Something to drink?" She chuckled. "Your ass can't even drink liquor," she said.

Zack waited until she got close. He shook his head and looked up at her as she spoke.

"If I did want a drink, I can't count on you to get one for me. Hell, there are some places you probably can't even get into."

"Queen, you trippin'," he said.

He reached out for her arm. Marleeta snatched it from his clutch, but she didn't miss the sudden rush of electricity that ran through her. "You need to push up, Zack, I got things to do. And I can't do them with you hanging around," she said.

"So that means you don't wanna go have a drink? That's what you saying?" he challenged, unmoved by her claim of things to do.

Marleeta put her hand on her hip. She rolled her eyes at Zack, then sucked her teeth. "Look, I ain't got time to be messing around with you. I'm not playing now, I got things to do," she said again.

She wanted nothing more than for him to get up and leave. Then her mind started to betray her. As his fingers worked the buttons on the remote control, it started thinking of other things those fingers could work.

"First I stroke the cat, real softlike, with the very tips of my fingers." Marleeta shook her head as if that was enough to make the thoughts of their road trip conversation disappear. *"I use my fingertips to spread the lips open, you know, that way I can go straight to the clit."* Damn, was he double-jointed in his fingers? She zeroed in on his hands as he flipped through the channels again. "Boy, you need to get up outta here!" she screamed. The conviction she used was enough to scare herself, but Zack only looked up at her. He glanced back at the TV, then erected himself and moved to the edge of the sofa.

"You really mean that? You want me to leave? 'Cause I ain't got to beg nobody. Trust me, there are tons of bit—I mean, women—who would give anything to spend time with me. And, honestly, I can only think of a few who are around my age," he said. When he licked his lips, Marleeta felt her knees tremble.

"So I take my tongue, and I place it right on top of the clit. I just sit there for a few seconds, so you can feel the heat and soft pressure from my tongue." She shot Zack the most evil look she could muster. "Look, you need to bounce," she said through gritted teeth.

After Zack had reluctantly left, Marleeta leaned up against the locked door and released a huge sigh of relief. What the hell was she doing, thinking about some young dick, and acting like she didn't have an ounce of sense? Shit, that young boy was a double taboo—not only was he young, but, shit, he worked for her!

Damn, I really need to get some dick. I'm up here thinking about molesting one of my workers. I know times are hard when I got to stoop that low, she thought.

And Marleeta did have things to do. It was dark outside, so she went into the shed she had built and removed the rug that covered the thick plastic tarp. There she had a safe buried in the ground. She quickly opened it, deposited the money, then locked things up and walked back to the house.

Since Stoney, she didn't really have a steady man. Yeah, there were a few she could call when she needed a little tuning up, but she wasn't looking for nothing hot and heavy. Marleeta was determined not to have any strings attached, 'cause in a few years she was planning to make a clean break.

She envisioned a life near the beach in her dream

house. She'd hire some locals to help her keep the place clean, and she'd travel back to the States about twice a year. But truth be told, she didn't need to do that. Hell, if all went well, she'd find herself some big-dick "Mandingo" and train him to slide his tongue up and down her clit, just like that young boy Zack had described. Marleeta looked around at the fence that separated her from her neighbor's property. The neighborhood was nice, nothing upscale or fancy, just hard-working people who were able to carve out a piece of something to call theirs. She'd sell the house when she left, 'cause she didn't want to have to deal with any needy-ass tenants.

After she walked back into the house, she figured the night was still young. She'd have some of the food Tamara had left, then kick back and watch a movie or something. What she really wanted, though, was some dick. *It's a good thing that young boy got his ass up outta here. I might've had to teach him a thing or two.* Marleeta started flipping through the pay-per-view movies. She selected one she wanted. She had fifteen minutes before the movie was set to start. She ran back into the kitchen, grabbed some of the food, then went and pulled the file on JD. *Now, this is the motherfucka I should be kicking it with right here.* There was nothing new in his folder. There were no new pictures or statements about his holdings; she just wondered what it would be like to have his tongue rubbing up and down her clit. Then she wondered if he'd be able to follow it up with a hard, stiff dick. Shit, she wasn't in the mood to masturbate again, she wanted the real thing.

Marleeta tossed the file, picture and all, to the

side; then she went to find her address book. The first name that caught her eye was Reggie, a big red-bone dude, with a long tongue and a nice-sized dick. Yeah, she'd call Reggie and invite him over for dinner. She didn't know where the hell she'd get dinner from, but she figured once he was here, he wouldn't care that the only thing she had for him to eat was her pussy.

She dialed *67, then his cell number, and waited for it to ring. After several rings, and no answer or voice mail, she hung up and redialed. This time, she was careful, thinking she must've messed up the first time.

"This is Reggie's phone. Who are you and what do you want?" a female voice barked.

"Ah, this . . . is—is Reggie available?" Marleeta asked. She didn't know why she was stuttering. Shit, she was calling to see if he was free, not to marry his ass or have his kids.

"He in the shower. Can I tell him who's calling when I join him?"

Marleeta hung up. Well, there goes that idea. Her movie, the remake of *The Honeymooners,* with Cedric the Entertainer and Black Hollywood's current It girl, had already started. But her mind was elsewhere. She flipped through her address book again, wondering how many of the men she used to be able to call on were now attached. The last thing she needed was drama. So she closed the book and eased back into the sofa. Suddenly she popped up on the sofa, then started scanning the room for the Yellow Pages. An idea struck out of nowhere.

She found the phone book and flipped to the

escort section. Marleeta had never done anything like that before, but, shit, it was ten forty-five on a Friday night and she was contemplating another intense masturbating session, or calling for some dick. She decided to go with the dick.

Marleeta almost slammed the phone back onto its stand when the woman asked what she was in the mood for.

"Ah, I need someone," she said.

"Yes, an escort, right?"

"Yeah. You got any black men?" she asked.

"Light-skinned, dark, muscular, atheletic type—is the event formal or what?"

"The event? Oh yes, um, this is, like, a last-minute thing. I need someone, like, in an hour. Is that possible?"

"Lady, anything is possible. Okay, so in an hour. Do you have an age preference?"

"Oh yes, I need someone thirty or older, but no older than forty-five. And I don't care about his skin color, as long as he's athletic. He can dress casually," she said, thinking about stamina.

"Okay, good, let's see what we've got available. Yes, we've got someone here. Byron is his name. Where would you like him to pick you up?"

"Um, ah, have Byron meet me in the lobby of the Four Seasons downtown."

"Okay, that's downtown LA, the Four Seasons. How would you like to pay for the services this evening? We accept all credit cards, we can do an electronic check or cash. Well, we only reserve cash for our repeat customers. Next time you'll be able to use cash."

"I've got a card. I need Byron to meet me in the lobby near the bar," Marleeta said. "In about an hour and a half. Is that okay? I know it's late."

"We can accommodate that."

Marleeta gave the woman her credit card information and told her she'd be wearing a red wrap dress with her hair in an updo. As soon as she got off the phone, she rushed to her bedroom, threw up her hair, put on the red dress, and hopped in her car. She was about forty-five minutes away from downtown.

With nearly thirty minutes to spare, she rented a junior suite and posted herself in a chair near the bar. Marleeta figured she needed something to calm her nerves, so she ordered a glass of Hypnotiq from the bar, then came back to her seat.

At 12:45 A.M., a clean-shaven man approached the chair Marleeta sat in. "You must be LeeLee," he said.

She looked up into his dreamy brown eyes. "That's me," she said.

He presented a white rose. "Byron at your service." He smiled.

Marleeta looked him up and down. He was close to six feet tall, not thin, but not husky either. He had on a pair of tan slacks and a navy button-down polo shirt with long sleeves. He looked good enough to eat.

After spending an hour in the hotel's bar, Byron didn't ask where they were headed. Marleeta wondered if enough time had passed before leading him up to the room. Another two glasses of Hypnotiq later, she no longer cared.

"I got a room for us, up on the sixteenth floor," she said.

His smile told her, he was down for whatever.

"Then what are we wasting our time down here for?" He rose from his bar stool. "Bartender, we're ready for the check," he said.

"Oh, they'll just charge it to the room," she said.

Byron pulled $20 from his pocket and left it on the bar as they walked out with drinks in hand. The second the elevator doors closed, Byron pinned Marleeta up against the wall. "Damn, you are so sexy," he said. He started sucking on her neck.

Marleeta started grinding her body into his mid-section, until she felt what she was looking for. He was hard. Damn, why was this elevator moving so slowly? She peeked to see they were just at the seventh floor. Nine more to go, she thought.

Marleeta used her free hand to explore his body. Beneath the shirt, she felt muscles and a hairy chest. She reached for his crotch, to confirm what she thought she felt. The grip she gave wasn't as large as when she held Zack, but she could definitely work with what he had. *Shit, the twelfth floor?*

By now, Byron was humping her so hard, she felt his belt buckle digging into her belly. Oh, she wanted him in the worst way possible. He couldn't get up off her soon enough when the doors opened on the fourteenth floor. Two men with name badges stepped on, and looked in their direction. Marleeta was so embarrassed; she grabbed Byron by the hand and hopped out of the elevator just before the doors closed.

"Let's take the stairs," she said. They looked around in both directions, until they spotted the stairwell. Byron led the way.

Marleeta was only allowed three steps before

Byron reached under her dress, pushed her panties to the side, and shoved several fingers inside her.

"Emph" was her response to the sensation. There was nothing gentle about his movements. He jammed his fingers deeper into her, forcing her back to the stairs.

"I wanted you the second I laid eyes on you," he said. He pulled the dress open and clawed at her bra. When that didn't work, he bit at the lace cups that held her breasts. Marleeta scratched at his back, rubbed his head, and tried to spread her legs farther apart.

After Byron used both hands to gather her breasts, which spilled from the still-fastened bra, Marleeta threw her head back and noticed a small camera in the corner of the ceiling. "Oh shit, we're being taped," she hissed.

But that didn't stop Byron, or slow his pace. *"Emh-hmm"* was all she heard.

Byron reached into his pocket, removed a black-and-gold wrapper, placed the tip of the package between his teeth, and pulled it open. He quickly slipped on the condom and thrust himself into her with great force.

"Damn!" Marleeta wanted to tell him to slow down, be gentle, but the more he moved his hips, the more she decided she liked his rough edge. She was so hot between her legs, she burned as he moved in and out of her. Each time he entered her, again, was harder than the last time. Trying to match his vigor, Marleeta flung her leg against the rail and used her hands to push his ass into her midsection. Byron humped her like a madman.

"Good pussy," he cried as he humped. "Good pussy."

"Oh yes! That's it," Marleeta cried. "Right there!"

Way too soon for her, he cringed, then grabbed her by the neck. She was a bit startled at first, until she heard him utter, "I'm, ah, I'm coming, babe. I'm—"

Before he could finish speaking, he had lifted her up from the stairs, grabbing her hips, and shoved her pelvis into his midsection. "Damn, I'm coming," he cried.

Marleeta didn't come just then, but she got so much pleasure from his outburst, she held on as his body shivered in convulsions.

She Works
Hard for the Money

Target: Johnny Freeman, aka Twin
Holdings: partner in two spas (brothels) in Denver, a modeling center in LA, a fleet of sports cars (six in all), two 2009 Mercedes SUVs
Estimated street net worth: unknown, estimated at 35 million
Drop schedule: unknown, suspected to move cash every week from spas & center
Security detail: None!!! Very friendly. One right-hand man, Rick (possible target)
Weakness: aspiring actresses and wannabe models
Misc: loves women in skimpy clothes

Nikki turned around again. This time, she moved slowly, allowing Twin's eyes to take in her voluptuous body. This was the second meeting she'd had with him. The first was during an open-casting call he held at the Marriott, near the Denver International Airport. Here they were, back at the same hotel again. But this time, Nikki had to try and get his attention.

No doubt about it, Twin was doing big thangs in Aurora and the Denver Metroplex. She had no idea how Queen did it. Zack had said Queen got his name off an arrest docket of all things. The mass arrest happened last year, back during the first or second week in December, something like thirty people were arrested in the major sweep in Denver. Queen was a badass bitch, that's for sure. She had a list of the thirty names and exactly what they were charged with.

Twin was charged with two counts of attempts to distribute crack cocaine. But Twin said he wouldn't be down for long, and he wasn't. He was free on bail before Christmas and had been living large ever since, like he ain't facing something like sixty years in the pen and nearly half a million in fines.

Just thinking about all that money made Nikki horny, and Twin wasn't even that much of a man. He was tall and thin, no body to mention. He wore his hair pulled back in a long, wavy ponytail that touched the middle of his back.

Queen said his twin brother died when they first moved the business out to Colorado from LA. That was years ago, and since then, Twin had been on the grind, stacking major cash and dabbling in legitimate businesses.

When they first met, someone asked about the charges he was facing, and Nikki heard him say he paid his lawyers good money so he didn't have to worry about such things. This was what Nikki was thinking about as she paraded in a skimpy bikini in front of him and his boys. She had passed herself off as an aspiring actress and model who wanted to work for him.

Nikki was one of three girls who were called back for follow-up interviews. Twin nodded, and she was escorted to a side room to change. Before she left, another man tapped her on the shoulder.

"Say, Ma, Twin wants you to meet him in room 432. Here's the key. You can order room service if you like. He said, make sure you shower," he added.

When Nikki walked into the room, she pulled her cell phone out and checked in with Queen. She looked around as her phone rang.

"Hello?"

"Hey, Queenie, I did it. I'm in his hotel room," Nikki said.

"Why the fuck are you calling me? You need to concentrate on the job at hand. He could have the room bugged, for all we know."

"Look, I was just checking in is all—"

"I don't need you to check in, just do your job. And don't fuck him. You need to know where he keeps his stash," Marleeta scolded before she hung up in Nikki's face.

"Ooooh, I can't stand that bitch!" Nikki screamed as she threw the cell phone. Just then, the door opened and Twin walked in.

"Damn, shorty, whassup with the temper tantrum? Who stole your sunshine?"

Nikki tried to regroup. She didn't expect him to come up so fast. "Oh, I'm straight. I didn't even have a chance to hop in the shower yet." She smiled at him.

"Oh yeah, that's cool, I just needed to come up and relax anyway." Twin reached down and picked up the cell phone and the battery, which flew off when it hit the wall. "Lemme see if I can put this back together. Remind me never to get on your bad side," he joked.

Nikki pointed toward the opened bathroom door. "I'm gonna go take that shower now," she said.

"Cool. I'll make some calls while you do that."

In the bathroom, Nikki turned on the shower but stayed by the door. With her ear pressed against it, she listened to Twin's conversation on the phone.

"Yeah, all I'm saying is that nigga better show up with all my money. It's been too fucking long."

There was silence for a few minutes. Then he started talking again. "Where you tell him to meet us?" Twin asked. "Yeah, Saturday is cool, but instead of there, I want him to come to the spot on Alameda. I want to be in familiar surroundings, you feel me?

"Cool, Saturday night at eleven-thirty, yeah, and tell that nigga he bet not think about being late. I ain't got all night to wait on his punk-ass either."

Nikki searched her purse for something to write with. "The spot on Alameda, eleven-thirty, Saturday night," she mouthed without making a sound. Frustrated, she dumped the contents of her purse on the counter and picked up her eyeliner pencil. She pulled a square of toilet tissue and wrote the details down. Then she folded it neatly and placed it inside her compact. She quickly jumped in the shower and prepared for her night with Twin.

"Don't fuck him!" She heard Queenie's voice ringing in her head. Nikki shook it off as she lathered her pubic hair with moisturizing shampoo. She lined herself up with the razor. Nikki rinsed under the shower's pelting water. About twenty minutes after the shower started, she turned the water off and stepped out. She dried quickly and used the hotel's lotion.

When she finished, she folded up her clothes, placed them in a neat pile, and walked out of the bathroom.

"Ah, I need to call you back," Twin said into his phone, taking in the sight of her glorious body. "Damn, shorty, you not shy a little bit, huh?"

Nikki ran her hand along the length of her body, starting from her shoulder to her thigh. "What do I have to be shy about?" She shrugged and turned full circle, giving him a good view of her ass.

"*Daaaayum!* Your shit is tight fo' sho!" Twin said. "Say, bend over and touch your toes," Twin said, getting all excited.

Nikki turned back around, spread her legs, and bent over to touch her toes.

"That's what I'm talking 'bout! You's a badass bitch, believe that."

A few minutes later, she felt his warm, wet tongue slopping her pussy's lips. After making a few slurping sounds, he kissed her ass, then rubbed his pelvis area against her ass.

"Damn, you even taste good too. Just a mouthful of joy, shorty."

Nikki stood up, turned to face him, and dropped to her knees. She stuck her hand into the opening of his boxers and took out his dick, which had sprung to life. She started planting light kisses on the head. She looked up to see him squeal in sheer delight.

"Talk about a mouthful," *kiss, kiss,* "of joy," *kiss, kiss. "Emmm-hmm,"* she hummed as she tried to deep throat him. Hardly able to contain his excitement or his strength, Twin started backing up toward the couch.

"Damn, ssss-hortyyy," he hissed. The more he

inched backward, the more she hobbled on her knees. For every two steps he took, she followed, with his stiff dick still hanging in her mouth. When he finally made it to the couch, he collapsed back onto his ass, and she pounced on him. She sucked, and sucked, then slopped, and sucked some more. Nikki was trying her best to suck every ounce of juice from his dick.

"Aaah, girl, you good. Real good," he cried.

She felt his body jerk. He grabbed the back of her head, holding her in place while she sucked harder. Just when his warm fluids began to erupt, she sat in his lap and felt his dick explode. Technically, she didn't fuck him, she thought as he lay snoring next to her. Nikki would've been asleep too, but lately her thoughts were all about the massive loss she suffered at the blackjack table two weeks prior. She needed money in the worst kind of way, and she was willing to do whatever she needed to get back to where she was.

Even two weeks after her loss, she still couldn't understand how she let $150,000 slip through her hand, as if it were boiling hot water.

Seven days after Nikki had given Twin the very best head he'd had, to date, the two were inseparable. He treated her like a queen, and she sucked his dick wherever and whenever she thought he wanted it sucked. Even at stoplights. When Saturday night rolled around, she was hoping all would go as planned. Nikki had never been so nervous about a job before, but she needed to score, because this was the closest she'd come to being broke. That scared the hell out of her.

At about 10:30 P.M., when they left the Lime Cantina, on Larimer Square in Denver, she could only pray they were headed to his spot on Alameda. Nikki tried not to appear twitchy, but she couldn't help second-guessing herself. She wondered if the GPS device was going to work. It hadn't failed since they started using it.

She wondered if Twin could've somehow changed his plans and not let her know. But, hell, she wasn't supposed to know about the original plan anyway, so there was no need for him to notify her of any changes, if things had changed.

Nikki really wanted to call Queenie, but she decided against that, thinking Queenie would only succeed at either pissing her off or making her even more nervous.

"Yo, shorty, what's up over there?" Twin asked, taking his eyes off the road briefly.

"Just a little tired, babe." She smiled.

"Well, I got some business to take care of, before we can chill for the night. Look, I was planning to drop you off, but I'm pressed for time and can't be late. So I hope you don't mind tagging along," he said.

"Naw, babe, I'm straight, whatever you want," she answered.

Twin raised his brow, and gave her a devilish smile. Nikki knew that was her cue to put her head in his lap. He even started unzipping his pants.

Later, at about ten minutes after midnight, Nikki lay naked in Twin's bed. Or the bed in the room of the house he wrapped up his business in. Either way, he had told her to get undressed and wait for him in the room. He said as soon as he cleared the house of all those niggas, he'd be all hers. She just wanted him to hurry. The last thing she needed was the boys busting in while she was tucked away in bed and Twin was up front with backup.

A few minutes after that thought, Twin walked into the room. "You still awake, shorty?"

"Emm-hmm," she purred.

"Good, 'cause I'ma fuck you girl, like your back ain't got no bone," he said, stripping out of his clothes.

"You promise, Pappi?" Nikki teased.

"Just wait and see," he said.

Nikki threw the covers back, revealing her naked-ness. Twin jumped on the bed. First he licked her thigh, then her navel, and back down to her mound. Nikki spread her legs as wide as she could.

"You strapped?" she whispered.

"Yeah, shorty, I'm straight."

He raised her legs and cradled them in the corner of his elbows. Without warning, he slammed himself into her and held himself really still. Before he could get his rhythm going, the bedroom door came crash-ing to the floor.

"Nigga, I'ma put lead straight up your ass if you even think about moving!" the voice said.

Nikki felt Twin's hips gyrating. That's when she saw the barrel of the gun sticking out of the back of his head. "I said, don't move. Get up outta that cat, but keep your hands where I can see them."

Twin did what he was told. He looked at the masked gunman, then at the one posted at the door.

"Make this easy, you know what we here for," the gunman at the door said.

"Shit!" Twin spat.

Nikki pulled the covers up to her chin and started sobbing.

The gunman turned to look at her. "Don't start that shit. This ain't got nothing to do with you. As a matter of fact"—he motioned to the other gunman—"tie her ass up," he demanded.

"No!" she cried. "I won't do nothing. Please just leave me alone," she said.

"One more word. Just one more, and I'll make you sorry," he warned.

Nikki sucked up her tears and prayed Trey wouldn't tie her hands too tightly.

Target: Rick Powell, aka Shadow
Holdings: partner in two spas (brothels) in Denver, a modeling center in LA, two sports cars, 2009 Mercedes SUV
Estimated street net worth: unknown, estimated at 2 million
Drop schedule: unknown, suspected to move cash every week from spas & center for Twin
Security detail: None!!!
Weakness: aspiring actresses/wannabe models
Misc: Twin's right-hand man, loves women in skimpy clothes

Across town, Tamara was sitting in the passenger seat of Rick's Mercedes SUV. He had taken her along while he picked up what she was certain was money from two spas. They had left the spot on Alameda nearly two hours ago. She caught a glimpse of Nikki going into the back room, and shot her a dirty look. It was what targets expected women to do. On the rare occasion that they bumped into each other while working a job, they acted as though they loathed each other.

By 3:00 A.M., Tamara was ready to get the show started. When Rick pulled up to the Marriott near the airport, she breathed a sigh of relief.

"I told you we'd wrap things up. Here, help me take these bags upstairs, and we can relax."

By "relax," she knew he meant *fuck until she was raw*. Rick's dick was the size of a horse's. And for the very first time, Tamara felt herself not looking forward to getting some dick.

Unfortunately for her, Rick was rock hard the moment they walked into the room. She dropped the cloth bag next to the door and he quickly scooped it up. He stashed it, along with the other three, into the closet in the bedroom and immediately started attacking her.

"I been waiting all night for a piece of you," he said as he reached down and sucked a spot on her neck. She stepped back. "Hold up, Daddy! I ain't going nowhere, but let me go take a leak first. We got all night, right?"

Rick rubbed his stiff dick and said, "Okay, yeah, you right."

Tamara slipped into the bathroom and pulled the heated K-Y jelly from her purse. She used the applicator to insert a generous amount into her pussy. She counted to ten, then walked out. It was no surprise that Rick was naked and sprawled out on top of the covers. His dick stood pointing upward with a slight bend toward the left. Tamara swallowed hard.

"Why don't you hop on," he said.

Tamara didn't know what to say or do. His dick looked like another leg. It could've been attached to a midget's body and it would've been right at home. She had never in her life seen a human dick so large, and he wanted to put it inside her!

"Um, you got, ah, um, a condom?" she asked, already knowing the answer.

Rick glanced down with pride, then looked up at Tamara. "Girl, when they make a condom to fit this, you'll be the second to know. Now come on over here and hop on. I wanna see you ride this." He beamed.

She was trying unsuccessfully to stall. "Okay," she sighed.

Tamara slowly stripped off her clothes, hoping the one-eyed monster would shrink a little. But when she looked up, it was still as massive as the first time she laid eyes on it. And with that little bend to the left, it was almost like it was staring at her, almost daring her to hop on.

"You ain't scared, are you?" Rick finally asked. He stroked himself, and Tamara noticed his massive hand couldn't even close around the member. The sight of it didn't make her feel any better. She felt even worse when she saw him roll the condom on because she knew there was no turning back now.

When she couldn't put it off anymore, Tamara bit her bottom lip and climbed up on the bed. After that, she swung one leg over Rick, then looked down. She sighed once again, then took him into her hand. She bent it toward the right, then put the head at her opening.

"Oh shit, girl, you are soaking wet—just the way I like it," Rick said, oblivious to her hesitation.

She felt full, with just the head of his dick at her vaginal lips. Tamara wiggled her hips and tried to suck more of him inside. She had never been stretched so wide. At first, despite the wetness, she still felt pain as he began moving his hips to help fit himself inside her.

"C'mon, girl, that's it, you almost there," he cheered.

Tamara wiggled some more. *Another two inches.* She released a breath, prepped herself, and wiggled her hips a bit more. *Okay, that has to be a good three inches.* She bit her bottom lip, used her hands to guide her down farther, and knew he had ventured to an area no other man had been able to go before.

"Whew!" Tamara said. When she tried to straighten her back, a piercing pain shot from deep in her pussy to the pit of her belly, forcing her to hunch back over.

"Take it easy, girl. I ain't going nowhere. You'll be a pro at this before you know it," Rick said.

Tamara began rolling her hips. It felt like his dick was tickling her tonsils, but she was determined to ride him. She didn't want to think about what would happen if he was on top. She didn't even dare move up and down on this gigantic pole. It was all she could do to slowly rotate her hips.

A few minutes after getting into a good slow rhythm, without the initial pain she had experienced, she had to fight the feeling. But her body wouldn't listen, she began to feel the tingling sensation in the tips of her toes.

"Oh shit!" she cried out. "I'm about to come, baby! I'm not ready yet!"

"Girl, your body's saying something else. Give in to it. We got all night. Do your thang. Do your thang with this sweet, tight little pussy of yours," he egged on.

The sudden outburst was like nothing she had ever experienced. Here it was ten, maybe fifteen, minutes into her ride and she was ready to throw in the towel.

She couldn't find the words to say she had had enough. She didn't want to fuck anymore. She came so hard, she started getting a headache.

"Naw, baby, it don't even work like that," Rick said as Tamara started to collapse next to him. "We just getting started." He turned her over on her stomach and she jumped up, screaming.

"No! Not like that, I can't handle it like that," she said, squirming to move beyond his reach.

He grabbed her by the shoulder, and she couldn't move.

"Naw, baby, you did your thang, now it's time for me to handle mines." He grunted and shoved her head into the pillow.

Smack!

When he slapped her ass, tears fell from her eyes. "Now hold still, I ain't got time for no games. I don't fuck with teasers."

"Ohmigod!" she cried into the pillow. Tamara realized that was only his finger, and her heart sank to her stomach.

All of a sudden, with no warning, Rick slammed into her. She screamed as loud as she could, fully crying like a baby. But her cries only fueled his fire. He lifted her midsection and grabbed her waist.

Tamara tried to wriggle free, but he was too strong for her.

"Ugh! Ugh!"

She managed to turn her head to the side. "*Plllleasse* stop, please. I can't take it."

'Ugh! Ugh!" he grunted.

The jelly she used the first time was gone, and with every stroke, she could feel the rawness of her flesh.

The more she cried out, the more he pushed. When he got tired of hearing her wimper, he slammed her head back into the pillow.

"Oh yeah, this little pussy is nice and tight," he said.

Tamara was bawling at this point. She was certain she was bleeding, but nothing stopped him. He continued to slam himself into her and hold her in place, to take all he had to give.

Again Tamara was able to angle her head to the side. She screamed, "You're hurting me! *Plllease stttop!*"

"Nigga, can't you hear?" the voice asked. It took the barrel of a gun to do what Tamara's cries were unable to do. Rick immediately stopped.

"You sure you want to do this?" Rick asked calmly, without moving.

"Search the room," the gunman yelled.

The other gunman looked under the bed, walked to the door, and yelled for someone to search out there.

"Bingo!" he said after he opened the closet and saw the four bags neatly stacked on the floor.

"Cool, grab 'em," the first gunman yelled.

The one who held the gun on Rick instructed him to get up real slow. He looked over and noticed Tamara was crying. He looked at her, then back at Rick. He used the gun to pistol-whip Rick until blood started flying around the room.

Tamara tried to pull herself together, but she was sore and in pain. "Please let me go. I don't have nothing to do with this," she pleaded.

The gunman looked at her. "Get the fuck out!" he said as he smacked Rick with the gun again.

Tamara grabbed her clothes, threw them on, to the best of her ablilty, and hobbled out of the room. She didn't care what happened to Rick. She wanted to ask if she could get a few blows in. As she walked out, she heard the sound of tape being ripped off its roll.

Regroup

Headquarters

At their hotel in Denver, Marleeta waited up for her workers to check in. Nikki had called to say her shit went off without a hitch, but she hadn't heard from Tamara or the boys. This was the first time they pulled off a connected double.

They knew Twin was doing big things in Denver, but through her research, information popped up that his right-hand man, Rick Powell, made the majority of his pickups. That's when they decided it would be best to hit them both. The minute Nikki confirmed that he kept that room at the Marriott, they knew they'd pull it off. She already had a key card. Nikki gave it to the boys, and it was just a matter of wait-and-see.

After they hit Twin up, the boys had less than thirty minutes to make it to the Marriott. The only thing they didn't know for sure was if Rick would take Tamara back to the same room. They were betting he would, and when he did, they struck gold.

Four plane tickets were reserved for them to fly

from Denver International to LAX the very next afternoon. As was routine, Zack and Marleeta would hit the road, to bring back the money. This time, they'd only spend sixteen hours on the road.

Once everyone checked in, those flying went to the airport. Zack and Marleeta made a beeline for I-225, and drove the three miles to I-25 north. There was no conversation in the vehicle. Zack was bouncing to his 50 Cent CD, and Marleeta was focused on the information in JD's folder.

By the time he turned onto I-70 toward Grand Junction, Marleeta had read over the information five times. There was nothing there she hadn't already memorized.

Zack reached over and lowered the volume. He didn't speak right away, but he waited to see if Marleeta would look up from the folder. He knew exactly what she was up to. She had become uncomfortable around him; for him, that was a sign of her weakening.

"So, Queenie, you get somebody to wax that ass yet? Don't think I didn't notice the bounce in your step when we got here to Denver. Like I said, I may be young, but I ain't no fool."

Marleeta kept reading.

"I know you ain't gonna try to ignore a nigga. Baby, this 'bout to be a long-ass sixteen hours," Zack said.

Marleeta had noticed a difference in him too. He seemed pissed, like he couldn't believe she didn't want to let him hit it. She couldn't picture herself with this little young boy. Yeah, Zack knew how to bring the heat, and he pulled off stickups like he was born to do 'em. But, shit, that didn't mean she needed to go mixing business with taboo sex.

Besides, the next time she felt like dropping several grand for some dick, she was sure she could hook up with Byron again. By the time she paid for their bar tab, room, the extra for him staying all night—and she supposed the sex—the total was just under four grand.

She had never had such rough sex before. If she hadn't, there was no way she would've known how good it was to have it rough. One thing she didn't expect, though, was the way she felt after she saw the credit card statement. She felt like one of those desperate women who *had* to pay for sex.

In the time she had been ignoring Zack, Marleeta had made a decision. It was time to hit JD. The others were right, she didn't know why she was holding out, but she figured she needed to get it over with. Marleeta knew exactly how she'd do it. She'd make sure she set up two other jobs, two days apart. She'd keep Nikki and Tamara busy then; the next day, she'd handle her business. As soon as they got back to LA, she needed to get busy.

She already knew a few of his local spots, so she'd show up and look around. After a few visits, she'd reel him in, then knock his ass off. Marleeta was getting all hot, just thinking about getting close to JD.

Zack glanced over just as Marleeta closed her eyes. She ran her fingers over JD's picture, then exhaled.

"I know you ain't over there creaming over that nigga," he said.

Marleeta's eyes snapped open. "I'm doing research, if you don't mind."

"Research, my ass. Wait, hold up! I know that's *not* the nigga you saving the cat for, is it? *So* you won't let me hit it, but you want that old head," he hissed. "You a trip, Queenie, a straight trip." Zack chuckled. "I ain't tripping, though, 'cause I know what's gonna happen. You building that nigga up in your mind, and when you do get down with him, you gonna be disappointed. But don't even worry about it, 'cause I'll be right here to make up for his shortcomings."

"Do you ever stop talking about yourself and how you can fuck or eat pussy so well? I mean, really?" she asked, looking at him.

"Queen, it ain't even like that. It's not like I go around talking to females about my abilities. But I'm feeling you is all I'm saying. And I know you all sexual and shit, and I know I can make you feel real good." He shrugged. "I'm just looking out for you. Shit, I know the stress you under. I'm just trying to help," he said.

"Yeah, while helping yourself, right?"

"Well, what kinda nigga would I be if I didn't look out for myself too? The truth is, Marleeta, we'd make one helluva team. That's all I'm saying," he said.

"We're already a team, or did you forget?"

"You know what I'm saying," Zack countered.

When Marleeta couldn't take the conversation anymore, she reclined her seat and eventually dozed off. She had a dream that she was fucking Zack on a private beach outside her house in Belize.

Zack woke Marleeta up as he pulled into a gas station the minute they got off the I-10. He didn't want to leave her sleeping in the car alone, with all that money, and he needed to piss like a racehorse.

"We there yet?"

"Naw, just a piss stop. You need to go?" He asked.

She stretched and yawned. "Actually, I do. You go first," she said.

"Naw, baby, why don't you go while I fill up, and I'll go when you come back," he offered.

"Sounds like a plan," she said. Marleeta got out of the car and stretched, long and hard. It felt good to walk around for a few minutes. Depending on traffic, once I-10 turned into Highway 101, they had less than an hour left on the trip. As usual, Marleeta called a meeting for the next evening.

As she walked toward the bathroom, Zack yelled, "Let me know if you need help wiping."

Marleeta stuck her middle finger up at him and sashayed into the gas station.

Playin'
with Fire

"I don't see why we gotta spend our fucking Friday night with her lonely ass," Nikki snapped.

She had plans to spend a few more hours in the Normandie Casino. Instead, she was sitting in Marleeta's living room, next to Tamara, who was acting like she didn't want to be bothered.

Nikki had to actually leave the blackjack table, just when she was up ten grand. She had this burning feeling that this could've been her lucky night for sure. Ever since she lost all that money, she had been on a serious mission to recoup her losses. And she knew, *you can't win, if you don't play.*

"Sssssh," Tamara warned.

"No, this is bullshit! How she just gonna make us go out with her. Hell, she didn't even care about whether we had plans. This is *bullshit*!" Nikki hissed. She rolled her eyes at Tamara. She couldn't understand why Tamara wasn't the least bit bothered by Queenie's latest stunt.

"I don't care. The way I see it, she's our boss. So, if she says we need to kick it together for a few hours, then I'm down. Queenie does a lot for us," Tamara challenged.

"You sound like a chump!" Nikki spat. "You act like we can't make it without her ass. We do all the damn work. Shit, she wouldn't be able to make it without *us*!" Nikki sulked back on the sofa. She pulled herself up. "Then she got the nerve to have us come over here and she ain't even ready. Oh, this shit has got to stop. Queenie needs to know, my time is my fucking time, not hers to do with what she wants, just 'cause she lonely and ain't got no man!"

Tamara shook her head and picked up a *Jet* magazine from Marleeta's coffee table. It had been nearly a week since they returned from the last job. Marleeta felt like she needed to do something to bring everyone together. She planned to have them spend the evening at the Century Club, in Century City. Everybody who thought they were somebody went to the Century Club.

When Marleeta stepped into the room, she looked over at Nikki and Tamara sitting on the couch. She was wearing a skintight Versace slip dress, with spiked stiletto heels and huge diamond studs in her ears.

"You look good, Queenie," Tamara said. She smiled and walked toward the kitchen. "I'm about to get a refill." She pushed her glass up. "Anybody want more?"

Nikki's face looked like she had sucked on something sour. Marleeta didn't miss her foul mood, but she told herself to ignore it.

"When are we going?" Nikki barked. She rolled her eyes and folded her arms across her chest.

"I ordered a car to pick us up, so the driver should be here in about thirty minutes," Marleeta said. She walked over to her entertainment center and turned on her Ja Rule CD. "That oughta put us in the partying mood," Marleeta said, ignoring Nikki. She took her drink and walked back into the room.

"Girl, I think we're gonna have a good time at the Century Club. I heard all the ballers be up in there," Tamara said as she sipped from her drink.

"That place ain't nothing but a big ole warehouse, with a bunch of fucking people crammed inside like sardines. I don't wanna go!" Nikki said.

"Well, I can't wait to get my groove on. Shit, we need to take some time out to party. Who knows? You might actually have a good time, Nikki," Tamara said.

An hour after they arrived at the private party being held at the Century Club, Marleeta, Nikki, and Tamara were out on the patio. They were people-watching from their table next to the outdoor dance floor.

Nikki kept nervously looking at her watch. Tamara was dancing in her chair. Marleeta just emptied their third bottle of Hypnotiq. The music was pumping and the crowd had spilled out onto the patio. They had been in the sushi restaurant on the balcony earlier, but they decided to post on the patio.

"Where are we going next?" Tamara asked, trying to spark conversation at the table, despite the music.

Marleeta shrugged her bare shoulder. "I'm looking

at something on the East Coast, but you know that's a helluva ride back home," she said.

"Well, I ain't trying to go back to Denver for a while. I just keep thinking that fool Twin might put two and two together about the room key," Nikki tossed in.

That had been happening quite a bit lately too. Each time Marleeta would toss out a city, Nikki would try to chime in with something negative. But on payday, it was all gravy.

The kick under the table was a little harder than Marleeta liked. But when Tamara did get her attention, and she saw who Tamara was looking at, Marleeta was grateful.

It was as if the crowd cleared a path for him as he walked out to the patio. An entourage of three other men surrounded him, but he definitely stood out. Nikki looked at Marleeta, then followed her stare to JD. Some little groupie had stopped him a few feet from the door. He was definitely suave.

Dressed in a coal-colored Armani suit, he looked clean. JD's smile was sparkling white, his fingers were well manicured, and his jewelry was tasteful. JD was speaking when his eyes wandered over to their table. For a brief second, he made eye contact with Marleeta, who blushed, then quickly looked away.

"*Emph,* I think I'm about to walk around," Nikki announced. When she got up from the table and walked, her low-rise jeans showed off her best asset, and she didn't have problems swinging it for everybody to see.

It was like he called her over, because she went

directly to JD. She took his hand and pulled him out to the dance floor.

"What the fuck is she doing?" Tamara asked. Marleeta didn't answer; instead, she kept her eyes on Nikki and the way she was wiggling all over JD. He swayed slowly to the music, but Nikki turned around to put her big ass right up against him.

"What have you decided about him anyway, Queen?"

Marleeta shrugged. "I just want to make sure our timing is right. He ain't the one to fuck up on," she said, still staring as Nikki was now bent over and shaking her ass. Still, JD only swayed, smooth and cool. Marleeta liked his style. As JD danced, his boys stood near the sidelines of the dance floor. They watched Nikki's every move on the dance floor.

"You see how his boys are on him like hawks. We gotta be able to plan for that. That's all I'm saying," Marleeta said.

When Nikki turned back around to face JD, she was visibly sweating. When she went low and lingered at his crotch, Marleeta closed her eyes and shook her head.

"She's making a fucking fool of herself," Tamara said.

After a few more seconds of the freak show, one of JD's boys stepped up and whispered something in his ear. While Nikki danced herself into a frenzy, JD pulled a BlackBerry from somewhere and started pushing buttons. He still swayed to the music as he checked the BlackBerry. Soon after that, he tapped Nikki on the shoulder, said something to her, then turned and walked out the way he had come.

Nikki shrugged, like it was his loss, then started moving to the music toward the inside of the club.

"That's what she gets," Tamara mumbled. "You gonna step to her?"

"I'll handle it" was all Marleeta said. With JD gone, they went back to their people-watching, and Tamara started swaying once again to the music.

About an hour later, Nikki returned to the table on the patio. Soaked, she was out of breath. She looked at Tamara, then at Marleeta.

"I know you guys haven't been sitting here the whole time, have you?" Nikki looked at Tamara. "What the hell did we come to a club for? Shit, we could've sat on our asses at the house," she said as she grabbed her glass and took the bottle of Hypnotiq from the ice bucket. "Hmm, if I knew you guys were gonna be so damn exciting, I would've come clubbing a long time ago," she said sarcastically.

"Why you step to JD like that?" Marleeta asked.

"Shit, somebody had to. I say that nigga is ready. You see how he was all over me. Shit, he couldn't stay away from the ass. I should've known he was an ass man. Most niggas are. Shit, some of 'em prefer ass over jumbo titties," Nikki said, like she was trying to convince them and herself.

"The point, Nikki, is, you know Queenie's been working on him—" Tamara began.

"I don't know no such thing. All I know is he's ready and we sitting up acting like we scared to step to the nigga." She looked at Marleeta.

"It ain't my fault if someone's treating him like he untouchable. He just another target, as far as I'm concerned. So we need to start acting like it and make a move. I'll bet he won't forget me. Shit, I think I need to work that one," Nikki said, moving back in her chair.

"Nah, I'm handling that one," Marleeta said calmly.

"Why? It's like you scared of him, or something. I say he should be up for grabs. You saw how he was all over my ass!" she spat.

"Until things change, I'm running Headhunters. Not you, Nikki, not Tamara or the boys, me"—Marleeta pointed at her chest—"and I say who we move on, and when. If you don't like it, then you can just find something else to do."

Marleeta got up and stormed away from the table. She wasn't sure why she was so bothered by Nikki's little antics. She knew the girl was just trying to challenge her. The reaction was probably exactly what she wanted, and Marleeta had given in. She also didn't know why she was hesitating with JD. She kept telling herself he was too close to home. They didn't usually work so close to where they laid or played.

By the time Marleeta made it back to the table, her mind was made up. It was time to move on JD and let the chips fall where they may. After going to the restroom, she had scanned the club but saw no traces of JD. She knew he was gone. The sinking feeling she had was hard to describe. She should've been the one to pull him out, the way Nikki did. She wasn't mistaken— they had made eye contact. And when they had, she got that same electricity flowing through her, like the time she touched Zack.

She and Tamara watched as Nikki continued to

have sex on the dance floor. She was working up quite a sweat, and making a spectacle of herself. Every once in a while, Tamara looked on, shook her head, and chuckled.

"Let's get outta here," Marleeta said. She had had enough drama for one night. What was supposed to be a relaxing evening of fun had turned into yet another confrontation with Nikki. She and Tamara got up to leave. Nikki spotted them and left her partner on the dance floor.

"Whassup? I know you guys ain't ready to go," she said. "Shit, the party is just getting started."

"Yeah, well, we've had enough," Marleeta said.

"Tamara, I know you ain't ready to go. C'mon, let's stay. Queenie is a big girl. She can make her way back home. She ain't 'bout to do nothing but go home to an empty bed. C'mon, girl, let's stay," Nikki begged.

"Nah, I'm good. Shit, I'm a little tired anyway. I say we bounce," Tamara said.

Nikki looked at Marleeta with disgust in her eyes. Marleeta glared back.

"What you gonna do?" Marleeta asked.

"Shit, I'm staying. You dragged my ass out here— now, just when things start popping, you wanna go, 'cause ain't nobody asking you guys to dance. Hmmm, I'm staying. I'll catch up with you guys later!" Nikki said.

"Suit yourself," Marleeta said. She turned and walked away.

Nikki shook her head at Tamara and returned to her dance partner.

"That bitch is playin' with fire," Marleeta mumbled.

"What?" Tamara asked as she jogged to catch up with Marleeta.

"I said, somebody's gonna get burned, real soon."

All Work
and No Play

Two weeks after the outing at the club, the Head-hunters had pulled off three successful jobs. Marleeta was more than ready to make her move on JD and had placed herself in his path twice since seeing him at the club. Both times he had taken notice. But as soon as he tried to step to her, she managed to disappear.

Tamara had started contemplating what her plans should be when they finally made up their minds to get out of the game for good. She thought Marleeta's plan was a pretty good one. They'd been talking about it more—especially since Marleeta was looking over the blueprints for her dream house. That alone got Tamara hyped.

However, Tamara couldn't imagine living anywhere but in the United States. She promised Marleeta she'd go visit, but she needed to keep her butt on U.S. soil. She didn't know anything about Belize, but most of those small countries probably struggled. Tamara wasn't trying to take her struggle anywhere else. She was thinking about buying some rental property. She just had to find a way to set it up without alerting Uncle Sam about how she made her money.

Unfortunately for Nikki, the Normandie Casino was eating up her money just as fast as she was making it. And if that wasn't enough, she had planned a trip to Vegas. She was more determined than ever to branch out. The only money she had to look forward to was from the most recent job. It's what had her driving feverishly down Central Avenue, heading to Marleeta's house.

Nikki was contemplating asking for a loan, but she thought better of it. She didn't need anybody all up in her business. She was running late and was mad at herself for stopping to buy a sheet of scratch-offs. Who would've thought spending $100 on scratch-off lottery tickets would've only pulled in $17! What the fuck could she do with seventeen funky-ass dollars? She wanted to go back to the convenience store and bitch slap the man who had sold her the damn tickets.

As she pulled up in front of Marleeta's house, she was thrilled to see Tamara getting out of her car across the street. Nikki wasn't in a hurry anymore. Before Tamara could think about crossing, Nikki ran to her car.

"Hey, girly, what's going on?" she asked. Nikki grabbed one of the food trays Tamara had sitting on the hood of her car.

"Nothing much. What's shakin' with you?" Tamara asked before she ducked back in her car to pull out more food.

Nikki didn't know why Tamara felt the need to

waste her money on food for the group each time they met. But she didn't care about that. She was hoping to finally convince her about a job they could pull off by themselves. Shit, if Nikki could do it alone, she would, but she knew she couldn't. She at least needed to pull Tamara in—that would increase her chances of getting one of the guys to go along.

"I've been thinking," Nikki said.

"Oh?" Tamara grabbed the second tray of sandwiches and a brown paper bag.

"Yeah, I finally came up with a way for us to make a little extra cash on the side. You down?"

Tamara sighed. She looked over at Nikki. "I don't think we should be talking about this right now. I mean, Queenie is expecting us. They waiting for this food, you know?"

Nikki didn't want to show her disappointment right away. The truth was, her plan was far from ready to be executed. She just knew in order to get Tamara on board she had to start working on her early. She had never seen such a kiss up in her life. She just knew the girl's breath must smell like shit, the way she stayed up in Queenie's ass.

"Well, what about when we leave here? Why don't we go somewhere, so you can at least hear me out? And if you don't like anything about my plan, we can change it. That's the good thing about working for, ah, um, I mean, with me. We can agree on everything before we make a move," she offered.

Tamara looked toward Marleeta's yard. "Aeey, Queenie, I got the food you wanted." She smiled.

Nikki wasn't sure how long Marleeta had been standing in her doorway, and she told herself she really didn't give a damn either. Truth was, she was tired of how cautious Marleeta was. It was costing them money, and she was tired of feeling poor. Especially as much as she worked, it made no sense.

"Shit, I was about to send out the cavalry," Marleeta joked.

Just then, Trey appeared at the door behind her. "C'mon, Tamara, we starving in here," he said. He walked around Marleeta to take the tray from Nikki. "Wassup, Nik?"

"You dawg," she answered. Yeah, it would be Trey. That's who she was gonna try and reel in to pull off her plan. She didn't know what was up with Zack, but she had a feeling he wouldn't think of doing anything without Marleeta's stamp of approval. And Danny Boy was just as caught-up as Zack. Yeah, she'd focus her attention on Trey.

One thing for sure, she was planning to split the money an equal three ways. Now, if that wasn't enough to convince them that they could make a killing real fast, she didn't know what would. Nikki wondered just how long she'd have to sit through Marleeta's idea of bonding as a team. She just wanted to pick up her money and jet out. Instead, they'd talk about the last job, how it could've been different, and what they should expect for the next one. If she was running things, they'd spilt the cash the night they pulled off the heist. Why sit on people's money? Shit, let them be responsible for getting their own cash back.

Who's to say Marleeta wasn't fudging the numbers anyway? Yeah, she usually took an extra ten or twenty right off the top, but Nikki felt like that should float. One job she gets it, the next Tamara, then Marleeta. But no, on each job, it was like Marleeta paid herself an extra bonus, like she got her ass out there and did some work. She didn't know why everyone was looking at her.

"What?" she asked.

"Queenie just asked you a question. What, are you sleeping with your eyes open over there?" Tamara asked.

"Oh, my bad. My mind was somewhere else," Nikki countered.

"I asked, how did you feel about a job closer to home?" Marleeta said, rolling her eyes.

"It's about time—" Nikki said, but Marleeta cut her off.

"Well, we're headed to Riverside one night, then it's Pasadena the next, and I'm taking JD on in Moreno Valley," Marleeta said.

Several eyebrows shot up, and it had nothing to do with the fact that they were staying close to home. Marleeta was going back out there.

It's about damn time, Nikki thought. Before she could control herself, she said, "Why do you get JD? I mean, the way he was digging me at the club, I think I should get a stab at him."

Marleeta looked at Nikki. Tamara looked at Marleeta; still, Nikki waited for the answer to her question. When Marleeta didn't answer right away, Nikki jumped raw on her. She stood up. "Anybody at the club could see how he was digging me. Once he saw all this ass, he was like . . . shit, it was like he was blinded. Some niggas just prefer the ass, and I know he's one of 'em," she said. Nikki was pleading her case. "It's like when we know a nigga is into skinny broads, we send Tamara in. When they prefer light skin, I'm on the job. If the nigga had a thing for big titties, then I'd say, 'Yeah, Queenie, go for it,' but he's an ass man." Nikki looked around the room. "And let's face it," she said as she turned and made her extra ass jiggle, "this is the mother of all asses."

Tamara closed her eyes and shook her head.

Marleeta looked up at Nikki. "Are you done yet?" she asked. Her voice was calm and steady. "Like I was saying before, I'm handling JD, and if anyone got a problem with that, then they can get the fuck out. I run things around here."

The guys looked around like they were bored. Tamara wanted to evaporate. And Nikki couldn't believe Marleeta was pulling rank on her. If she didn't need her money in a serious way, she'd walk the fuck out. But her trip to Vegas depended on the cash from this job. Maybe once she struck it rich in Vegas, she'd dump the entire crew. She'd organize her own clique and make a killing on her own. But for now, she knew she needed to sit still.

Yeah, she'd let Marleeta try to take on JD, but when that shit blew up in her face, she'd be right there to say, "I told you so."

Hours after the meeting, and everyone had been paid, Tamara sat on Marleeta's living-room couch.

"I don't know what's going on with that girl, Queenie," Tamara said. They were sipping on mimosas.

"I ain't worried about that chile. I wish I could replace her ass, but, shit, it ain't like we could just run out and get another big-booty bitch . . . like, 'Oh, we have an opening in that department, you wanna interview for the spot?'"

"Yeah, well. I don't think we need to go to that extreme. Honestly, I think she's going through some shit right now. I don't know for sure, and I don't even know if it's true, but I suspect she is," Tamara tried to reason.

"Well, that may be the case, but I'm getting a little tired of the challenges. When I started Headhunters, I thought I'd be working with two other like-minded females. Instead, I always gotta worry about what she's gonna have to say when I make a decision. That shit is starting to wear me out."

"I don't know what's gotten into her. You want me to talk to her?" Tamara offered.

"Naw, don't even worry about it. Let's just get the work done, make this money, and move on. Like I said, it ain't like I can replace her ass, so I'm not even gonna worry about it. At least she don't mind taking care of business when necessary, and that's all that counts really."

"Okay, cool," Tamara said.

Since they knew JD liked the Century Club, that's where they were headed. Marleeta didn't waste her time telling Nikki about their plans, since she was so pissed about having to go last time.

This time, when they stepped into the club, Marleeta spotted her target right away. JD sat at a booth surrounded by bottles of champagne, a couple of his homies, and several women.

When Marleeta walked over to the group, everyone stopped to stare, including Tamara. "What are we celebrating?" Marleeta asked as she looked directly into JD's eyes.

JD's eyes swallowed her up. They went from her French-manicured toes, which lay flat on the stiletto heels, to the diamond anklet glistening on her left ankle. They traveled up her caramel-colored muscular legs and lingered at her jagged hemline.

The mocha-colored suede miniskirt stopped right in the middle of her thigh, where the tiny words *slippery when wet,* with an arrow pointing upward, sat. He smiled at that, and looked at her diamond belly-button ring, her four-pack, and again his eyes traveled to the matching strapless top she wore. Her breasts flowed over the top. Marleeta let her fingers linger right at the crest of her cleavage. Her other hand was placed seductively at the side of her hip.

"We celebratin' you and me finally hooking up, boo," he said.

The women sucked their teeth at her audacity. The men stroked their dicks on the sly.

"Why don't we go somewhere a little more private," she said as she reached for a glass. "So we could get to know each other better." Marleeta smiled and helped herself to a bottle from one of the numerous ice buckets standing near the booth. "You know, without all these distractions," she tossed in, throwing back one of the several nasty stares she got.

JD was damn near speechless. He knew he liked her style already. And he also knew exactly who she was but he was intrigued by the mystery and danger that surrounded her. The Queen Bee herself coming in and all but calling him out.

"So what's on your mind?" he asked, finally finding his voice.

"Well, I have a car waiting outside. I like Redondo Beach myself," Marleeta said.

"Damn, you mean, you trying to take a brotha out? I'm not even used to that," JD said, all but pushing a hoochie up off him. "Here, why don't you come sit for a few minutes so we can talk."

Marleeta sipped the champagne and shook her head. "Nah, Daddy, I don't ever do crowds. It's just not my style." Some of the champagne dripped as she moved the glass from her lips. She used her index finger to wipe the fluid and allowed the finger to sit in her mouth for a few seconds.

"Damn, I wish I was that finger," JD said.

"Fo' sho," one of his boys chimed in.

Marleeta chuckled. "I can't tell. I mean, it usually don't take this long for me to convince a man to let me holla at him for a few," she said.

Her first night with JD went well. They sat on the beach, talked, and sipped Hypnotiq, or at least she did. JD had Incredible Hulks, mixing his with Hennessy. By the time they finished getting to know each other better, the sun was coming up.

"Damn, look at that, boo," JD said, pointing to the burnt-orange ball that sat right on the blue line of water. The light it cast was a mixture of violet, orange, and gold.

"Yeah, that's tight," Marleeta said.

"Shit, girl, we been drinking all damn night. And I mean all night too."

"I know, we probably need to go sop this shit up with some pancakes and eggs," she offered.

"You cooking?"

"Naw, Daddy, but I know somewhere we can go and get our eat on, and it taste just like some real good home cooking." She smiled.

"Let's roll then," he said.

For the next three weeks, JD and Marleeta kicked it so much, she had access like they'd known each other for years. He was so comfortable around her, he even conducted a few business transactions in her presence.

Marleeta was just buying her time. She wanted to do this right. Part of it meant she couldn't allow him to know exactly where she laid her head. It was hard enough with him thinking she was in the import-and-export business. When he asked what that was all about, she told him she mainly worked the phones, connecting clients with things they wanted. When he asked about the kind of "things," she lied and said trinkets, sometimes rare antique jewelry. That seemed to be enough to satisfy his curiosity.

JD didn't mind, he had told her he liked to keep his valuables real close anyway. Nearly a month and a half after their night on the beach, he looked up as she was preparing to leave. "Why don't you just move a few things in," he suggested.

Marleeta didn't expect that. She was completely unprepared. "Ah, baby, I ain't trying to cramp your style."

"I mean, think about it. You spend most of your time here anyway— all this running away every few days. I'm just putting it out there. And as far as cramping my style, you know I don't be sweating all these damn gold diggers that be jocking a brotha, all hard and shit. Least with you, I know you bringing in your own dough, so I don't mind somebody who trying to work with a brotha," he said.

Marleeta finally made it out the door and hopped into her ride. When she got around the corner, she pulled over for a few minutes to catch her breath. She wasn't sure how long she could go on with the lies. It was hard keeping up with what she had told JD. At one point, she told him she lived with her elderly grandmother and didn't like taking company to the old woman's home. On a different occasion, forgetting about the living arrangement lie she told, she mentioned having to pay property taxes. She was able to clean that up by saying that was the arrangement she and her grandmother agreed upon. When he didn't question her, she figured he was okay with what she had told him.

Back on the road again, she made a few detours before hopping on the freeway that would take her home. That was her way of ensuring she wasn't being followed.

The minute Marleeta stepped out of her car, her crew approached.

"What's up, Queenie?" Zack asked.

Marleeta jumped at first. When she saw all of them, she kind of felt like they were about to put on some kind of intervention. "Aeey, you guys, what's poppin'?" she asked.

As she unlocked the door, she noticed Nikki getting out of her vehicle. Marleeta figured she was late to the party, as usual. Once inside, she turned to find ten eyes staring at her. "What?" she asked.

Everyone looked at Tamara, but it was Nikki who spoke up. "Look, we don't know what the fuck is going on with you and that nigga JD, but the shit is starting to affect business."

Marleeta shrugged. "Oh? How so?" She looked at the rest of her crew.

Nikki flicked her hand to her hip. Her neck started rolling and her mouth was all twisted. "Well, let's see, for starters, we was supposed to see some action last night, but since Zack didn't hear from you, he refused to make a move. If he ain't moving, you know Danny Boy and Trey are, like, on froze. Then Tamara's ass was damn near beat down by her target's baby mama in some drama-type shit. We may have lost out on that job completely. And we ain't heard from your ass, ain't seen you." Nikki rolled her eyes. "This ain't no goddamn way to run no business is all I'm saying!"

"I hear what you sayin', but I was down and out for a couple of days. I caught a wind of that virus that's going around. Shit, I was in bed, barely able to move, so JD turned off my cellie so I could get some rest. But I'm back and poppin', so let's do this," she said.

"Queenie, I don't think you hearing me straight. Do what? I mean, we done lost out on Tamara's target, and, shit, I don't know if we should roll on mine just yet," Nikki said. Her tone had softened a bit.

"What's up with this nigga JD?" Zack asked. "I

mean, what y'all supposed to be married, and shit, now? He still on the radar or what?"

That was the same question Marleeta had asked herself hours earlier when she sat on the side of the road contemplating her next move.

Let's Get Busy

The intervention must've worked, because Marleeta was moving at record speed after the little "talk" the crew, or Nikki, had with her. Two days after they'd successfully pulled off the job on JD, she sat in her living room following the GPS tracking system on her computer monitor. She was on the phone with Zack as he drove to the location. "Okay, what does it look like out there?" she asked him.

"We straight. No security from what we see."

"Cool," she said.

"Okay, we 'bout to do this. We'll check back in, in about an hour," Zack said.

That hour wouldn't be easy on Marleeta. JD had already called twice, asking where she was and why she wasn't on her way over. She told him she had some family business to tend to. She was thrilled about Zack's call that finally interrupted their conversation. When she clicked back on the line with JD, after taking Zack's call, she said, "See, more drama. I need to run, babe. I'll probably get with you tomorrow or something."

"Naw, girl. You need to get back with me later tonight, I don't care how late it is. 'Sides, I got something real nice for you," he said. JD had been trying to make it up to her ever since the shit went down. He told her he wasn't worried about the money—that could be replaced. He was just glad she didn't get hurt. He would've doubled, even tripled, what those niggas took as long as they didn't hurt a single hair on her body.

Marleeta had set it off with JD. She planned and pulled off a romantic evening at his house in Moreno Valley. She fixed steaks, lobster tails, mashed potatoes, and a chocolate cake. They ate to candlelight and listened to soft music.

"Damn, boo, this was real nice," he said, looking around at the intimate setting. "Then you got rose petals sprinkled all over the place. This some ole magazine-type shit," he said, nodding approvingly.

Marleeta felt good. She knew she hadn't lost it, but she also had something to prove to herself and her crew. Even though dinner was the bomb, Marleeta wasn't near finished.

"You wait right here and I'ma go get dessert." She smiled.

"Cool. I'm just gonna move over to the couch and I'll be ready," JD said. When his cell phone rang, Marleeta picked it up. "This was supposed to be off. Remember? That was part of the agreement," she said.

"Just click that bitch off, babe. I must've forgotten. I ain't even worried about nobody trying to reach me right about now," he said.

When Marleeta stepped out of the bedroom, wearing a long white-laced nightgown that hugged her body like a second layer of skin, she saw his mouth watering. The push-up cups made her large breasts look even bigger. JD got up before she could make it to where he sat.

"You look so damn good! I'm ready to unwrap and eat my dessert right now," he said. His fingers lingered at her overflowing cleavage.

Marleeta wanted to mount him the instant he touched her. She pushed him back and sashayed past him. *"Ah-ah-ah,"* she said. "I've got a special treat. You'll get your chance to eat when I'm done." She walked back around to the front of the sofa. "So come take your seat and get ready for a show."

"You ain't got to tell me twice." JD walked around and plopped himself onto the sofa. The music changed. The beat was faster and louder.

Marleeta swayed her hips and popped her pelvic area to the beat. JD's eyes told her he loved every second of her dance of seduction. She was working it, and soon she noticed his dick was rock hard.

"C'mon, girl, I can't take it anymore," he whined, rubbing his crotch.

Marleeta took one of her spaghetti straps and flicked it off her shoulder. Still, moving to the beat, she held up the front of her gown and shimmied until the other strap fell. She wiggled her torso until the gown slid to her waist. With her arms covering her breasts, she shook her hips seductively, pulling JD in with every move.

When she walked up to him, she noticed a layer of perspiration across his forehead. Marleeta hiked up her gown and swung one leg to the left side of his body. Inches away from his stiff dick, she gyrated her hips to the sound of the music.

"I can't take it no more," he hollered just before he pushed her back onto the floor and took her breast into his mouth. "Damn, girl, you got me all twisted. I can't stop thinking about your fine ass." *Kiss, kiss.* "A nigga can't get shit done, 'cause you always on my mind," he said.

As he sucked on her neck, he slid his hand beneath the gown and fingered toward her thong. "You got me all worked up," he breathed.

Marleeta spread her legs and wrapped them around his body. They were so caught up in the throes of passion that when the door came crashing down, they barely separated.

"Yo, son, back up out of that cat!"

JD felt the barrel positioned to the back of his head. *Smack! Smack! Smack!*

"Damn, what you doing?" Marleeta screamed.

"Break yo'self, nigga. You know what the fuck we want! Don't make me get stupid up in here," the gunman hollered.

JD could barley steady himself. "I got you, dawg. Ain't no need to get stupid. I got you!" he said.

Marleeta had never seen a target so cooperative. He was calm, almost like he had been through it before. "Don't panic, boo. Let your man handle this," JD said to Marleeta.

Smack! "Nigga, ain't nobody told you to speak. Just get the loot so we can get the fuck up outta here!"

"You ain't gotta keep hitting on him like that!" Marleeta screamed.

"Bitch, I'ma hit yo ass if you don't shut the fuck up!" The gunman looked at one of his buddies. "Say, y'all take that nigga to the safe." He pulled a duffel bag out. "Make sure that nigga breaks himself. Smoke his ass if he tries anything, and I mean anything! I'ma stay out here with this one." He nodded toward Marleeta.

The minute JD left with the gunmen in tow, the gunman guarding Marleeta reached for and fingered her breasts.

"Don't touch me!" she hollered. "Remind me to kick your ass later," she then whispered.

"You need to leave these little-dick niggas alone and step up to the big leagues," he said, grabbing his crotch.

Marleeta shook her head and smirked. She pulled her gown over her head, giving the gunman an eyeful when her arms finally left her breasts.

After they left, JD held her close. He couldn't stop apologizing, saying he promised he'd always protect her. Marleeta kept thinking she had to get the fuck away from him. She didn't need to start getting attached. How the hell would she shake the nigga when she needed to?

Since then, he had called continuously. JD had piqued her interest, but she was in the middle of conducting business. She knew she couldn't just drop him; she didn't want to run the risk of raising his suspicion.

"I gotta go, babe." She didn't promise she'd call back, but left it open, depending on how the boys felt after Nikki's job.

Target: Charlie Patterson, aka Phat Cheese
Holdings: two apartment buildings in the heart of Riverside, two Hummers, two BMW SUVs
Estimated street net worth: 20 million
Drop schedule: every Friday
Security detail: travels with entourage, made up of family members, two known addresses, moves around regularly
Weakness: strong women
Misc: loves kinky sex

Nikki walked out to the balcony on the second floor of Phat Cheese's sprawling two-story house. She had been daydreaming about how much money she would've been able to rake in, had this been one of her jobs instead of a Headhunter's gig. This would've been the one to set her up nicely. Nikki wasn't sure how long she was gonna be able to keep taking orders from such an unstable bitch.

And that's exactly what she thought of Marleeta. Here they were—the boys, Tamara, and herself—working their asses off, and Marleeta had the nerve to be playing house with a fucking target! Now granted, they did take about a month and a half, sometimes more, to work the targets, but never as long as Marleeta was dragging the shit out with JD's ass. Nikki had a right mind to go and fuck him on the down low, just to teach her ass a lesson. But, shit, her Vegas trip was still riding on this. She had already told Marleeta she needed her money fast, 'cause she had some important business to take care of the minute that money hit her hands.

Nikki had decided she'd get paid, and then fuck JD when she got back from Vegas. She figured she'd really be rolling in the dough then anyway. So when she and JD got down, and he got sprung, like she knew he would, she'd be able to walk away from Marleeta and all her bullshit. Yeah, that's what she'd do.

"*Shiiit,* I better go make this money," Nikki said as she looked through the glass doors. Phat Cheese and his boys seemed to be in a heated conversation. She wasn't sure if it was the right time to barge in.

Damn, she wished like hell she could hear what the fuck they were talking about, but she couldn't. Nikki was hoping his boys would leave soon. She knew Zack and the crew would be headed to the house in the next hour. She had purposely told Zack to wait for an hour after the GPS displayed a static location. Truth was, she wanted to fuck Phat Cheese. Something told her he knew how to work those hips, and she wanted to find out for sure.

When Nikki tried to glance into the room without being noticed, her eyes locked with Cheese's right-hand man. He and Nikki already didn't get along, so she didn't think anything of it when he gave her the look of death. Shit, she only wanted some dick and some cash, and she didn't have time for some two-bit service-ass nigga to get in her way.

As far as Nikki was concerned, all men fell into two categories: shot callers and the niggas who serviced them. Phat Cheese was the shot caller, and his crew consisted of three niggas who serviced him in any way they thought he needed.

Nikki needed to piss, like R. Kelly on a sex tape, and she didn't have time to waste. She opened the door and noticed everyone stopped talking. She was from around the way, so she knew that meant she was probably the subject of the conversation, but, shit, she didn't care. If all went well, she and Phat Cheese would be fucking within the hour. She needed these fools out of there before Zack and the crew came bursting in.

Cheese looked up when Nikki walked into the room. "Whassup, baby girl?"

"Need the little girl's room," she said, quickly moving toward the spiral staircase that led to Cheese's private bathroom.

"So, um, I'll holla at you niggas later," Cheese said as Nikki reached the staircase.

The right-hand man stood. "Okay, dawg, if you sho you know whassup, just hit me on the hip if you need a nigga," he said. Nikki didn't miss the sideways glance he gave her.

As she walked up the stairs, Cheese's two friends left. Nikki was glad to see them gone. By her calculations, she had about thirty minutes to get a good fuck in before the shit went down. If all went as planned, she'd be headed to Vegas within seventy-two hours, and could be rich before the weekend was out.

Inside the bathroom, Nikki's head was spinning. *How the fuck could this shit happen? Now what?* She paced the bathroom floor and tried to avoid looking at herself in the mirror. All of the signs had been there— the cramps, the headache that wouldn't go away—but still her mind was on her nerves. She thought she was panicked because Cheese's boys were hanging around. Nikki took a large wad of toilet paper from the roll and tried her best to fold it into a neat pad. This had to work. She didn't know how she was going to break the news to Cheese, but she wanted nothing more than the thirty minutes to fly by.

The knock on the door nearly caused her to jump out of her skin.

"Hey, baby girl, what's up in there?"

"Oh, nothing, I'm coming," she said.

But before she could think straight, the door swung open. Phat Cheese stood there in his boxers and wife beater, staring at her and the wad of toilet paper in her hand. "Damn, shorty, what's going on in here?" He stroked his crotch. "A nigga need some release," he said.

Nikki started shaking her head. "I wish I could, boo. You know I want to, real bad. But, shit, my fucking period just came," she confessed.

Cheese shrugged and looked at her. "What's that got to do with me?" he asked.

Nikki scrunched up her face. "I said, I'm bleeding, nigga. I mean, damn," she said.

"Damn, my ass, baby. Don't act like you ain't never—"

"I'm just saying, I'm cramping," she said.

"C'mon, girl, you'll like it," Cheese said.

"I can suck you off to sleep, but ain't shit else happening," she said. Nikki turned to flush the toilet, and when she did, Cheese shoved her up against the vanity counter, tore off her panties, and shoved his dick deep inside her.

"Whha-at the fuck?"

He shoved the back of her head toward the marble countertop and continued to shove himself into her.

"Oooh yeah. See, I told you, this is the shit right here. You like it, baby girl?"

After a while, the sex started feeing good to Nikki. She realized Phat Cheese had a fat dick and he knew exactly what to do with it. It didn't take long for her hips to start matching his every move.

Suddenly she stopped. Nikki pushed herself into an upward position and looked at him through the mirror. "Let's take this to the living room. I want you to stretch me over the back of the couch and fuck me real, real good," Nikki said.

Cheese's hips were still moving slowly. "Is this what you want, baby girl?" he asked as he cupped her breasts with both his hands and started squeezing.

"Um-hmm," she cooed.

"*Sssssssss.* Wait, hold it right there," he cried.

Nikki couldn't help but clench her muscles. His dick was good, and she knew if they didn't stop right away, he'd explode soon. "C'mon, let's move this to the living room. I just wanna get comfortable. I wanna give you the fuck of your life, but this hard-ass countertop is killing me," she whined.

"I just don't wanna take it out, baby girl," he cried in a voice she had never heard.

"Trust me, you won't be sorry," she assured him.

As they walked out to the living room, a loud crashing sound made them both jump for cover.

The door had been kicked in and three masked gunmen rushed in.

"Don't move!" one shouted.

"Do exactly what they say, baby girl," Cheese said.

Nikki was too stunned at his calmness. She didn't understand how, and why, he would be worried about her during a time like this.

"That's right, bitch. Do exactly what we say and y'all might make it outta here alive."

Nikki was able to grab a pillow from the sofa, but it wasn't enough to cover her nakedness entirely. Her eyes darted between the gunmen and Phat Cheese, who had his hands in the air, as if the police had said "Freeze."

"Where's the dough, nigga?" the ringleader asked.

"Aeey, dawg, I don't hold shit up in here," Cheese said.

Gunman number two looked around at the lavishly decorated house. "Oh, you holdin' something up in this bitch. Ain't no doubt 'bout that," he said.

The ringleader put the gun at Cheese's head. "We ain't leaving here without your stash, nigga. So whassup?"

"Just give 'em what they want," Nikki said.

Suddenly all heads turned toward Nikki. Phat Cheese seized that moment of diversion. He overpowered Zack and grabbed his gun.

Target: Joe Lewis, aka Ozie Joe
Holdings: several businesses in San Bernardino, Hummers, sports cars
Estimated street net worth: millions
Drop schedule: 1st and 15th of every month
Security detail: two bodyguards and two familiy members
Weakness: women and money

Tamara didn't know what the fuck she was supposed to do. Deep down inside, she knew her time had come and gone. Where the fuck were the boys? Did something happen with Marleeta and she couldn't get in touch with Tamara?

This is what she thought as Ozie Joe spread her legs wider than she thought possible. He was abusing her pussy to the point of no return. Tamara had never had a pencil dick work with such precision. That little thing was hitting her walls, and the man attached to it was sweating like a bucket of water with a leak.

Every few minutes, Ozie Joe would blow his hot, sour breath in her ear and tell her to call his name.

"Oh, Ozie Joe! Yes!"

His little dick would just not stop. It kept going and going, and he was actually wearing her out. But what was getting to her more than anything was the way his wet body was drenching hers with all that damn sweat.

Once again, her mind wandered to where the hell the boys could be. The more she thought about them not being there, the longer it seemed like they were going at it. After Ozie Joe bust a nut in her, she wanted to run to the bathroom and dial Marleeta's number to find out what was going on.

But the instant he withdrew his lifeless dick, he wasted no time in dipping his head between her thighs and started gnawing on her clit. Tamara might've been able to survive the constant jabbing from his tiny dick, but when he cut loose with that winding tongue of his, she came so hard, she nearly pulled her own damn hair out.

Tamara had every intention of getting up and washing her ass, then calling Marleeta while the water ran, but she rolled over instead, satisfied and worn-out. She told herself she'd shut her eyes for a few minutes, then get up once she caught her wind.

The next time Tamara's eyes opened, the sun had been up outside, and Ozie Joe was not lying next to her. She could barely control her racing heart. What the fuck had happened to Zack and the crew? Why hadn't Marleeta called? Would she have to endure yet another night with this tiny-dick nigga?

Tamara walked toward the sound of voices. As she made her way down the long hallway, her mind kept flip-flopping about what excuse she'd have to use to get outta there.

"Okay, but you niggas done come up short again. I don't understand. We moving major firearms and ammo, and my money still ain't right? Somebody betta get to talkin'," she heard him scream.

Tamara peeked her head around the corner. What she witnessed nearly made her pass the fuck out. Ozie Joe was pacing, and three of his boys were sitting around, looking down at their hands. Between them and Joe stood a neat stack of crisp bills. Tamara had never seen a more beautiful and enticing scene in all her years. Her right hand started itching, her throat got dry, and her coochie was wet.

"Damn," she whispered. She needed to get on the ball. Tamara wondered where everyone was. Why hadn't anyone called to let her know there had been a change in plans?

Tamara crept back into the room. She wondered if Ozie Joe kept all that cash in the house. They could've struck gold, had they gone through with the plans the night before. *What the fuck,* she wondered as she sat on the edge of the bed.

After turning on the water in the shower, Tamara locked the door and pulled her cell out. She dialed Marleeta's number first. No answer. She hung up when voice mail clicked on. Next she tried Nikki— again, no answer. Tamara looked toward the door. She thought she heard footsteps, so she quickly stripped off her clothes and stood next to the shower door. The cell phone lay on the floor next to the pile of clothes and other items from her purse.

Shit, she needed a shower, but she also needed to

let somebody know they needed to move on this money. That pile alone could set them all up for good—no more jacking and robbing. *Where the fuck is everybody?* Tamara wasn't about to leave Joe's side until Zack and the crew ran up in there with guns blazing. Shit, she was ready to get paid.

When she heard the bedroom door open, she jumped into the shower. A few seconds later, Joe popped his head into the bathroom. "Damn, girl, you still in the shower?" He opened the door wider.

Tamara turned and smiled. She rubbed her palm against the steamed door and smiled at him.

"I'm 'bout to order some food. What you want?" he asked.

She shrugged. "Whatever you feel like," she said.

When he closed the door, Tamara quickly washed herself and stepped out of the shower. She left the water running. This time, she feverishly dialed Zack's number, then Trey's. By the time she got to Danny Boy's voice mail, she had a burning feeling something was definitely not right.

When Things
Go Wrong

When the call came in, Marleeta didn't know quite what the fuck to do. Should she wait around for them? Maybe she needed to try and find the boys to find out what had gone down. No, that couldn't work—she had to go. Nikki's screaming voice kept ringing loudly in her mind. And although she didn't have any of the details, something told her she needed to high-tail it out to Nikki's location, real fast.

"Oh shit, Queenie! They been shot!" Nikki had said.

"Who?" Marleeta screamed into the phone. "Who's been shot? Who?" she yelled before the line went dead.

Nikki had been screaming hysterically. She could barely utter another word. Marleeta had wanted to tell her to clean up what she could, and get the hell outta the house, but Nikki was so hysterical she couldn't understand how she was able to even call Marleeta. And why the fuck would she call, all crying about *they* got shot, and not say who the fuck *they* was?

By the time Marleeta arrived at the house, it was swarming with vehicles. No cops, no ambulances, just more cars than what had to be normal for that quiet area. Marleeta knew, because she couldn't find a place to park. Several vehicles were double-parked, others had hopped the curb and parked all over the well-manicured lawn. The one car she didn't see was Zack's. Marleeta didn't know if that was good or bad, but she also knew she wouldn't learn a damn thing by driving around and looking for a place to park.

She pulled up next to a black Mercedes G500 and left her car running. She didn't know what she'd find, but she had to go in and see what the fuck was happening.

As she strolled up the walkway, she could hear voices—angry, loud, growling voices.

"Bitch, you gon' tell us what the fuck happened up in here!" a man yelled.

Marleeta walked up and pushed her way into the house. The door wasn't locked.

"You gon' step back away from her, or I'ma put some hot lead up your ass," she said, pointing a nine-millimeter pistol at the man who stood over Nikki.

Nikki was shivering, nearly naked, and crying uncontrollably.

"Who the fuck are you?" The man turned to Marleeta.

"Don't worry about who the fuck I am. All you need to know is, I will shoot your motherfuckin' ass dead. I suggest you move up off my sister, and move real slow!"

When two men walked down the hall, they stopped cold in their tracks. Marleeta looked at them; they looked at the man who had moved away from Nikki.

"Y'all make one move and I'll kill his ass!" she said toward the others.

"What's going on?" The man spread his arms out. "You say this is your sister? We ain't trying to hurt her. We just wanna know what happened. My boy Phat Cheese is dead, baby. We just want her to tell us something"—he looked back at Nikki—"but she ain't been able to say nothing, just sitting there, crying." He shook his head. "When we left, we left her here alone with him. Then we come back and the place all tore up, and my nigga is dead! And she can't say shit?"

"Well, maybe that's 'cause she don't know shit," Marleeta offered. "I know she don't need nobody hovering all over her. You *see* she upset, probably scared, and shit." Marleeta kept the gun on him.

When one of the men started toward her, she looked at the man standing over Nikki. "I swear I will kill his ass if you take another step." She nodded toward the man. "Tell him I'm not playing," she said.

"Look, nigga, don't move, okay. We just trying to figure out who did all this shit, baby. Just calm down," he said soothingly. "It ain't no reason for you to be pulling weapons all out and shit." He shrugged. "I wanna kill those fools who did this to my boy and got your sister all fucked up in the head. That's all I'm saying."

Nikki looked up at Marleeta. "Queenie," she cried, like she just now recognized her standing there.

"Nik, go to the car!" Marleeta screamed as she steadied the gun.

The man started shaking his head. "We just wanna know who did this shit, that's all," he repeated.

Nikki scrambled up off the floor and ran out of the house.

"All I know is somebody robbed them early this morning. My sister called, crying hysterically, and it took me forever to find her. I don't know who did this to your boy. I didn't even know anybody was dead. I just needed to come find my sister and take her home. Just leave us alone, we don't want no trouble. I suggest you figure out who had a beef with your boy, and handle your business without us," Marleeta stated.

"I think it was them mafia fools. You know that fool Dizzy and Cheese had words the other day," one of the men from the hallway said.

Marleeta looked back at the man who had been interrogating Nikki. "I'm about to step outta here. I don't want no shit," she said.

"Go 'head, baby girl. This ain't got nothing to do with y'all. I just needed to know what happened to my boy. We gon' handle ours, you bes' believe that. I'm just sorry we had to meet like this, though, 'cause I could use a down-ass female like you. You straight—you real straight," he said.

Still holding the gun, Marleeta backed up out of the door and slowly walked down the walkway backward. Satisfied they weren't about to follow her, she hopped into her car and sped out of there.

Before making her way to Highway 91, she pulled off at a Holiday Inn Express. Nikki still hadn't stopped sobbing. Marleeta didn't know what to do about her. She knew the girl needed to calm down, but she didn't want to push her over the edge.

Once they walked into the room, Nikki started up again. "He dead, Queenie, he dead," she sobbed.

Marleeta was tired of hearing it, but she knew she couldn't just slap the shit out of Nikki, even though she wanted to. She only hoped that after they had a little time to relax, she wouldn't have to listen to the endless sobbing about Cheese being dead, especially during the hour-long ride back to LA.

Once they settled into the room, Marleeta put her head into her hands. She knew this wasn't the time for *her* to fall apart. She needed to know what happened during the job, and where the fuck Zack and the boys were.

Marleeta let Nikki sleep for about an hour. She ordered a huge lunch, then knocked softly on the bedroom door.

"Nikki?" she called.

When Marleeta didn't hear Nikki answer, she opened the door. Nikki was sitting on the bed. Marleeta couldn't tell how long she'd been awake.

"Why don't you take a shower, the food is ready," Marleeta said.

A few minutes after Marleeta closed the bedroom door, she heard the shower running. She felt good, hoping she'd be able to get to the bottom of what had gone wrong during the job.

"I didn't know what you might want, so I ordered a few things," Marleeta said.

"It don't matter, I'm just hungry," Nikki said as she sat and started going over the food on the tray.

Marleeta didn't want to press Nikki. Lord knows, she didn't need her crying again. After they sat eating for a few minutes, Marleeta looked over at Nikki. She sighed, then softly asked, "What happened last night?"

Nikki shook her head. "It was a mess up in there. I mean, you see people get shot on TV, but that shit in real life is crazy." She pointed to her ear. "My fucking ears won't stop ringing. I know he dead," she said. Nikki took a large bite of the steak sandwich. She shook her head again. "I just know he dead," she said. She picked up a few French fries and stuffed them into her mouth.

Marleeta leaned back. "Yeah, I'm sure that shit wasn't easy. Cheese is gone, but I need to know what happened. I mean, who even started shooting up in there?"

Nikki suddenly stopped chewing. Tears started rolling down her cheeks. "Cheese?" she said, sobbing. "I ain't talking about Cheese. He ain't nothing but a fuckin' target. Fuck that fat bastard. I'm talking 'bout Zack," Nikki cried out. "He got shot, I know he dead, and it's all my fault." She sobbed again. "It was all my fault, Queenie," she whispered.

Nikki didn't need any words to know she had pulled the rug from right under Marleeta's feet. Somehow the thought of that didn't bring her an ounce of pleasure. But it was true—all of it was true. It had, in fact, been her fault—the shooting, the mess, all of it. All she had to do was play her role. Instead, she had fucked up. She couldn't keep her mind off that money and the Vegas trip. She felt that as soon as they got the cash, the faster she'd be on her way.

Why did she have to say anything? The rules hadn't changed. Marleeta had told them, preached into their brains: *"Just play your role. Act your ass off, cry, think of something depressing, pinch yourself if you have to. Shit, do whatever it takes, just play your role."*

But Nikki had to urge Cheese to give 'em what they wanted. She just didn't feel like stretching out the stickup for hours. She had already made up her mind that she'd hang around till noon or so, then head back out to LA. She could be on her way to Vegas a whole day sooner than she had planned. But that nigga Phat Cheese was up in there, acting like a bitch over some cash. She just wanted Zack and the boys to get the cash and get out, but when she spoke, everybody was distracted.

When Cheese got the gun outta Zack's hand, Danny Boy didn't hesitate to start blasting. Cheese got off a couple of rounds before he went down. That's when Nikki started to help.

"Check the back, way in the back of the closet," she had yelled in the midst of all the confusion. She watched as they cleaned out the closet, taking cash and a few pistols. But as they were rushing out, just before they got out the front door, Cheese pulled himself back up.

"Zack!" Nikki had screamed. But she wasn't fast enough.

Cheese looked at her and started shooting up the place. Before Nikki hit the floor, she noticed someone with a mask got hit. The other two dragged him along with two stuffed duffel bags out the door. All she had to do was play her role, but she couldn't. For some reason, she just needed to make sure they knew where the loot was hidden. She didn't have time for the bullshit. Cheese didn't want to part with his money, and she wasn't about to beg for it.

From the moment the bloodshed went down, she sat in the corner, crying. She had no idea how she'd face Marleeta, or even Tamara. How would she tell them Zack was dead because of her greed? They'd been working jobs for almost two years, and in that time, there was never gunfire, and certainly nobody ever got shot, or killed.

Nikki just knew Cheese's boys were on their way. They already didn't like her ass, she should've left, but how? She managed to get her hands on her phone, hit the button that quickly dialed Marleeta, and uttered a few words, until she heard what sounded like cars pulling up outside.

Sunrise brought the wrath of Cheese's friends. Obviously, he didn't expect her to stay all night, because his boys were busting through the door right as the sun was coming up. When they saw all of the blood and destruction, they started grabbing their own guns.

Nikki looked up to see them staring down at her.

"What the fuck?" someone hollered.

"Rock, Toot, go search upstairs. Scott, Pink, y'all go to the back." It was the one who had mean mugged her earlier while she stood on the patio. Now he was shouting orders, sending everyone off on a mission before turning his madness on Nikki.

"I told that nigga not to trust your gold-digging ass. What the fuck happened?" he screamed at her.

Smack!

Nikki's face stung. She sobbed and cried louder. "He dead!" Her body shook uncontrollably as she cried. "He dead!"

"Yeah, bitch, who did this shit? What do you remember? What happened? And why did they leave your ass? This shit just don't add up!" he screamed.

Nikki flinched at the sound of his voice. She was

expecting to be hit, again and again. She had no idea how she'd make it outta there. Her mind kept playing the shooting over and over again in her head. She just wanted the images—the blood, the sound of bullets firing out of the barrels—out of her head.

What felt like hours later, something made him stop. He wasn't yelling anymore; he just stood and moved back. He held his backhand midair, bringing it down slowly to his side.

Nikki didn't dare look up. She should've been shot. She should've been the one to die, not Zack. It wasn't until the dude turned his back on her that she noticed Marleeta with the gun.

"You gon' step back away from her, or I'ma put some hot lead up your ass," Nikki heard Marleeta say. That's when Nikki knew for sure she'd walk outta there alive. She didn't doubt Marleeta would use the gun. She just hoped Marleeta and Tamara would somehow understand that if Nikki could, she'd trade places with Zack. If only she could.

Her ringing cell phone pulled her back to the hotel room, to the look of shock still on Marleeta's face. "I'm sorry, Queenie," she said.

"Where are they? I haven't heard from Danny Boy and Trey. You sure it was Zack? I mean, are you sure any of them got hit?" Marleeta asked. She reached for Nikki's cell phone and answered without hesitation.

"Hello?" she said, still looking at Nikki.

"Damn, it's about time! What's going on? What happened last night? Zack didn't show up. I've been trying to call you guys. What's going on?" Tamara asked.

"Girl, it's way too much to get into. Where are you?" Marleeta asked.

"I'm in San Bernardino. Where are you guys? What's going on?"

"We're in Riverside. I had to get us a room, we're right off 91, why don't you take a cab and come here. We need to talk," Marleeta said.

"Noooooo," Nikki cried.

"Is that Nikki? Why she crying? What the hell is going on, Queenie? I can't wait for no damn cab. Tell me whassup now!" Tamara hollered.

"Look, I don't need you getting all worked up too. Just get in a cab and come here. We'll talk when you get here," Marleeta said.

"Who keeps calling you?" Nikki asked.

"You know what—don't worry about all that right now. I need to figure out where the boys are, Tamara is on her way, and I need some answers before she gets here," Marleeta said.

"You're not about to leave, are you?" Nikki asked.

"I need to run out for a few minutes, I'll be right back," Marleeta said.

Where the fuck she be going right now? She know I ain't feeling right, and she 'bout to run outta here? Nikki felt like Marleeta was only concerned about herself. She was probably going to call that nigga JD. Nikki pushed the food cart back and went to lie down. She needed to rest herself, and get her mind off that madness. She just hoped Tamara would be able to find it in her heart to forgive her. Only time would tell, Nikki thought as she lay back on the bed and closed her eyes.

Close for Comfort

By the time Tamara's cab pulled up in front of the Holiday Inn Express, near Highway 91, she was a hot mess. She couldn't understand why Marleeta couldn't be straight with her over the phone, but she was determined to find out just what the hell was going on.

Before she could pay the driver, something caught her eye. Marleeta sat on a bench outside the hotel, and it looked like she was crying. *That can't be right,* Tamara thought. She paid the driver, then walked over to the bench.

"Ah, Queenie? What's the matter?" Tamara sat next to Marleeta. "What's been happening? I couldn't reach you, Nikki, or the boys," Tamara said.

Marleeta tried to pull herself together. "Girl, I'm so sorry. Um, Nikki . . . she's upstairs in the room. I hope she's getting some rest. We gotta take a break. Um, I mean, I just . . . I don't know how to tell you this," Marleeta said.

Tamara's head snapped back and her brow shot up. "Tell me what?"

"Um, there's no easy way to say this. But it's Zack," Marleeta said.

"Zack? My cousin Zack? What happened? Oh, hell no, what happened, Queenie? What happened?"

"I need you to calm down. I can't take all of this right now. I really need you to calm down," Marleeta said.

"You need me to calm down?" Tamara jumped up. "Okay, well, why don't you tell me what the hell happened to my cousin?" Tamara sat back down. "I'm sorry, Queenie, but cut the crap. What happened to Zack?"

Marleeta shrugged. "I don't know really," she said.

"Then why are you out here crying? What room are you guys in? I'll go ask Nikki. I can't take this shit," Tamara said. She got up and stormed into the hotel's lobby. She walked up to the front desk, then slowed her pace.

Marleeta walked up to her. "Just follow me," she said. They walked to the elevator. Marleeta pressed the button and waited for the doors to open. Inside the room, they walked into the bedroom, where Nikki lay on her back staring at the ceiling.

Nikki jumped up when they walked in. "Tamara, I'm so sorry. I didn't mean to do it," she cried.

Tamara looked at Nikki, then at Marleeta. "Do what? What the fuck did you do? What is going on? Where's Zack? I don't need to listen to the two of you crying. Shit! Somebody needs to tell me what the fuck happened!" Tamara hollered.

"I can't believe you didn't tell her," Nikki shot at Marleeta. "How could you bring her up here so I could break the bad news to her? You're a fucking coward!" Nikki spat.

Smack!

"Bitch, I've had enough of you and your shit. If you woulda kept your fucking mouth shut, we wouldn't be in this mess right now! How dare you call me a coward?" Marleeta shot back.

"I don't believe you slapped me! You don' lost your fucking mind," Nikki said.

"What the fuck happened to my cousin?" Tamara screamed.

Nikki and Marleeta both stopped talking. They looked at each other, then at Tamara.

"Zack is dead," Nikki said.

"He may be dead. We don't know for sure. Somebody got shot during Nikki's job last night. Zack, Danny Boy, and Trey—I keep calling, but they're not answering."

Tamara stumbled back to the bed. She put her hand to her forehead. "Let's go, we need to get back to LA and find them."

During the hour-long ride back to LA, Nikki and Marleeta filled Tamara in on exactly what had happened. The plan was to pull off three jobs in two nights. Marleeta and JD's went off without a hitch. Nikki's would've, but the shooting changed that. They just had to pass on Tamara's altogether.

When Tamara told them about the stacks of paper in the living room, Marleeta nearly turned the car around, but they all agreed. The boys were the most important thing. They set off to find out what had happened.

They pulled up in front of Marleeta's house and found Zack's car parked there.

"Oh shit, what are they doing here?" Tamara jumped out before Marleeta could come to a complete stop. She rushed to the driver's side, with Nikki and Marleeta close behind. They were stunned at what they saw.

It Clicked

In Moreno Valley, JD and his boys were sitting around and talking about the heist. Eddie drained his glass and got up. "Who you think did it?" he asked.

"I don't know. But them niggas were pros." JD nodded. "That shit went off without a hitch. They caught me slippin', that's fo' sho," he said.

"Say, you still make them tapes?" Charlie asked.

"Shit! I didn't even think of that," JD said, jumping up from his chair. "I started to stop the recorder, but I didn't get around to it."

The boys followed him into what he called his viewing room. There, they sat and watched the romantic evening JD had shared with Marleeta unfold before their eyes.

"Damn, she's one fine-ass bitch," Charlie said. He didn't catch the cross look JD tossed his way.

"Yeah, she is, but a nigga felt like a chump with the way that shit went down," he said.

"Oh, don't sweat that shit. We 'bout to figure out who them niggas are, and we gonna make 'em sorry they ever fucked with you, dawg," Eddie promised. "I put that on everything I love."

JD fast-forwarded the tape to the part where he and Marleeta were on the floor. His hand went up her gown, and then it happened. They sat back and watched as the gunmen entered the room. JD flinched as he saw the gunman smack him around with the barrel of the gun. "I wanna get them fools." He snickered.

When JD and two of the gunmen walked out of frame, Charlie yelled, "Hey, wait. Y'all see that shit? Stop the tape! Stop the fucking tape!"

JD used the remote to hit the pause button. "Whassup, dawg?"

"Look at how she acts when she's alone with that nigga. She don't look all that scared anymore. Now, see." He pointed to the images on the screen. "She turns her head toward the hall and says something, but he just kind of lets her do it."

"Whoa!" Eddie screamed. They watched as the gunman fondled Marleeta's breasts. It looked like she playfully swatted his hand away. She didn't seem disgusted or afraid.

JD replayed that part at least five times. "Aw, hell naw. She a cold piece, ain't she?" he mumbled, his eyes still glued to the screen.

"Dawg, volume. Can we turn this shit up a bit?" Charlie asked.

When the tape was rewound to the part right after the two gunmen led JD out of frame, he turned the volume up:

"Don't touch me!" she hollered. *"Remind me to kick your ass later,"* she then whispered.

"You need to leave these little-dick niggas alone and step up to the big leagues."

They watched in awe as the gunman joked with Marleeta, then grabbed his crotch playfully.

"See there," Charlie said. "Rewind. It looks like she laughing with that nigga—that's mad foul. Oh, she a cold piece all right. She needs to be dealt with!"

They watched again as Marleeta shook her head and smirked on the screen.

JD eased back in his chair. "So they know each other, if that ain't a bitch!" he said after he pressed the rewind button again. He watched once more as the gunman grabbed Marleeta's breasts. He had to save face in front of his boys, but inside he cringed as he watched her smile, then swat at the gunman's hand.

She helped them niggas rob me, then act like she was so terrified. Had me all worked up over the trauma I thought she was struggling through. JD nodded slowly as he watched the tape.

"I can't believe that bitch had me set up," he said.

"What you want us to do, dawg? We can find that bitch and make her ass sorry she ever crossed you," Eddie offered. "You know you my nigga, right?" he asked JD.

"Yeah, dawg, yeah," JD answered.

"Well, I say we handle this shit!" Eddie said.

"Oh, naw, don't even worry about it. I'ma handle this one all by myself. I want y'all to find out everything you can about her and her crew. But don't do nothing—not a fuckin' thing, you hear? Just bring the information back to me." JD's eyes narrowed as he watched her pull the gown over her head. It looked like she shook her titties for that nigga, right under his damn nose, right in his own fucking house.

Oh yeah, he thought. *It's gonna be real tight fixing her ass.* "I'ma show baby girl what it's like to play in the big leagues for real," he said.

"Believe that, son, believe that!" they all agreed.

He and his boys exchanged pounds as JD hit the rewind button again.

"He ain't dead!" Marleeta screamed as they stood outside the rented SUV and watched Zack's chest move up and down. Tamara started beating on the window. Zack and Danny Boy jumped up. Zack wiped the side of his mouth with the back of his hand and looked around. He pressed a button and lowered the window.

"Damn, where y'all been? Niggas fell asleep waiting on your asses." Zack unlocked the doors. He and Danny Boy got out of the SUV.

"Queenie, open up the house so we can get this shit inside." Marleeta, Tamara, and Nikki all stood with their mouths hanging open.

"Damn, what's going on?" Danny Boy asked as he tried to lug two of the duffel bags on his shoulders.

"C'mon, y'all!" Zack snapped at the women. "Shit, we need to talk," he added.

Inside, Zack told them how Trey was shot as they left Phat Cheese's house. He looked at Nikki. "Yo, that shit was foul. I don't know whassup with you and shit, but you supposed to let us handle our business and shit. You got my nigga all twisted, 'cause you didn't follow protocol."

"What happened after you guys left?" Tamara asked.

"Is he dead?" Nikki asked somberly.

"We don't know," Zack admitted.

"What do you mean, you don't know? Where the fuck is he? What happened?" Marleeta asked.

"Queenie, chill, okay? Look, just like you guys have plans for emergencies, we do too. We all agreed when we first started, if anybody gets shot, we drop 'em at the nearest hospital. That's what we did with Trey."

"I know you kidding, right?" Marleeta looked between Zack and Danny Boy.

"Nah, he ain't kidding. Drop at the emergency room door, that's what we did with Trey. Just like we agreed. We took off that nigga's mask and dropped him off," Danny Boy added.

Tamara shrugged. "So how we supposed to know what happened to him?"

"Just chill, we'll find out sooner or later," Zack said.

Marleeta couldn't get over how nonchalantly the boys were talking about Trey. He could be dying in a hospital and had nobody by his side.

"Just chill, Queenie. Trust, we got this. If Trey makes it, he'll holla and we'll go pick him up. It's that simple." Zack sat down. "Now let's take care of the business at hand. A nigga want to get paid so he can go chill for a minute," he said.

Nikki sat quietly.

"Yeah, I think we can all use a break," Marleeta said.

After the money was divided, no one rushed to leave, like they usually did. They all sat around. Even Nikki wasn't in any particular hurry. Normally, close to $100,000 in her pocket was like a free pass to the casino. Any casino.

"So what should we do?" Nikki asked, looking around the room.

"About what?" Danny Boy asked.

"I can't just sit here, not knowing if he's alive," Nikki snapped.

"Well, what do you think we should do? I mean, what if he's dead? Are you gonna explain to police how he died? You know they gotta report any gunshot wounds to police, right?" Marleeta asked.

"Who gotta report it?" Nikki challenged.

"The doctors, nurses, hospital staff. So when Trey comes out of surgery, he'll be handcuffed to a bed, and surrounded by the boys in blue, shooting questions at him like crazy," Marleeta said.

Nikki looked at Zack, as if she didn't believe what she was hearing.

Zack simply nodded. "The thing is, he supposeta say the last thing he remembers is riding in a car with his boys. Then when they ask his boys' names, well, he'll throw out Jon and Bob, no last names," Zack said.

"It's like ya'll got this all worked out," Tamara said.

"Aeey. Don't you guys have some stuff you do when things fall apart or go the wrong way? It's the same with us. And that's the plan. If it was me, I'd have to do the same," Danny Boy commented.

The group sat around and looked at each other. Marleeta thought she should've organized another one of her group events, but the truth was, she was not in the mood. After they all left, she would call and check on the progress of construction on her dream house in Belize. She'd send some money, and think about moving up her retirement date.

Marleeta didn't want to ask anybody to leave. She figured, since they were still hanging around, they were either waiting for the first person to leave, or they were still thinking about Trey.

"I'm so glad you not dead, cuz." Tamara smiled at Zack.

"*Shiiiit,* I'm glad too," Zack said. "You ain't got nothing to drink or eat, up in this bitch, Queenie?"

"Let's order pizzas," someone said.

Marleeta rolled her eyes, but no one was paying attention. She turned the radio on, since company wasn't trying to leave. They ordered pizzas, and she went into her private liquor stock.

"Say, Queenie, I'm probably headed to the Keys for a few days, you wanna come?" Zack asked.

No one tried to hide the perplexed looks on their faces. They all looked at Marleeta, as if they were waiting for her answer.

"Y'all wanna go to the Keys?" Marleeta asked.

Everyone shrugged. Zack looked disappointed, but truth was, Marleeta didn't want to go to no damn romantic island with him. Not to mention, *alone* with him. She still thought about his tongue and it rubbing up against her clit, but, shit, she wasn't about to be turned out by no young-ass boy and get sprung. She knew he was packing, and he knew that she knew. But for him to call her out like that, in front of everyone—oh, he was tripping for real, she thought.

Let's Chill

Three days after they'd been paid, and decided to take a much-needed break, Marleeta arrived home from the nail shop to a funny feeling. It was like someone had been in her house while she was gone. Subtle things started fucking with her. She knew she never left the cordless phone off the hook, *ever*. It was actually one of her pet peeves. But there it was, sitting on her coffee table, like that's something she'd do.

After she looked around the kitchen, then went to the guest bathroom, she knew for sure someone had been in her house. She had no idea who and why they had been there. The toilet seat was left up. Now, why would a single female leave the seat up? The last time she had company was several days ago, and she had cleaned the very next day.

A chill suddenly ran through Marleeta's body. In the three years she had been running the Headhunters, they hadn't had any problems. Now, suddenly, Trey was shot, and someone was creeping around in her house. She intended to get to the bottom of this shit, and quickly. During this off time, she was working on a couple of jobs for the next few weeks.

Everyone had said they weren't ready to retire just yet, and Marleeta felt like she didn't need to press the issue. Sure, they'd have to change the way they did things, but Marleeta felt being a little extra cautious couldn't hurt. But in the back of her mind, she had the feeling Cheese's boys might soon be on the warpath.

While no one else wanted to think about such things, Marleeta knew she wasn't about to become anyone's sitting duck. She considered sharing her fears with Zack, but she figured that wouldn't do anything but give the boy some false hope of getting in her panties. She also felt like the others wouldn't be able to think straight, until they heard something about Trey and how he was doing.

Tamara didn't go to the Keys with her cousin, but she was glad he wasn't the one shot. She knew that was a foul way to think, and deep down, she hoped Trey would be fine, but she didn't know how she'd survive if it was Zack or even Danny Boy who had been shot.

Instead of going to the Keys, she took a flight out to Houston. When they had worked jobs there before, she knew she wanted to eventually call the city her home. The cost of living was cheap and the houses were huge. Tamara had been talking with a developer about some property she was hoping to buy. Trey's being shot made her feel like the end was near, and she didn't want to be left holding an empty bag, with nothing to call her own.

When Tamara arrived at Hobby Airport in Houston, she took a cab to her hotel, then went to the Roulette Homes main office, off Westheimer Boulevard. The sales rep Gerald Smith met her in the lobby.

"Ms. Howard, good to see you again." He extended his hand.

Tamara took it and smiled. "I'm good," she said. "Thanks."

"I hope you haven't eaten. I made lunch reservations," Gerald said.

"I could eat," Tamara said.

They arrived at the Italian restaurant and breezed through a meal of lasagna and wine. When the waiter brought the check, Gerald presented his platinum card and turned back to Tamara. "Ms. Howard, I know you want to build, and we can certainly do that, but before you sign the papers, I wanted to tell you about some properties we have that are still brand-new. I think we can find something you might like."

"I don't have to build. If you have something similar to my floor plan, I wouldn't mind looking at it," she said.

"Great. The Royal Oaks Subdivision is new, with several unoccupied homes. We could get you in something for a reasonable price."

By the end of the meeting with Gerald, Tamara had a feeling she had found a home. She didn't want to move on it right away, but she did give Gerald and Roulette Homes a deposit of $20,000. The sprawling five-thousand-square-foot house was everything she could want, and she didn't have to build.

Her flight was scheduled to leave Friday evening, so Tamara went to the Wonder Bar on Thursday night. She had asked the black security guard where she could go to have a drink and listen to some music. The middle-aged black man was more than happy to steer her toward the Wonder Bar. Once Tamara arrived, she took a seat at the bar. It didn't take long for her to attract company.

"I'm buying the next round," a deep voice said as Tamara drained her glass.

The bartender nodded and went off to refill her drink. Tamara smiled. "Thank you, but you don't have to do that."

"Know when to let a man do something nice for you. What are you drinking anyway?" the stranger asked.

"Hypnotiq," Tamara said.

"Hmm, good choice. I've never seen you here before," he said.

"Are you here that often that you keep tabs on who comes in and who's new?" she asked.

"Aw, c'mon now, baby girl. I'm just saying, I probably come here about once a month or so, after work, to unwind. Sometimes I come Thursday, sometimes Saturday, and I see some familiar faces, that's all," he confessed.

Tamara nodded.

"'Sides, ain't every day I see a fox like you hanging around alone. *Shiiit,* you bound to stick out up in here. Look around," he offered. "Most of the regulars up in here are all tired and beat-up–looking."

After a quick glance around the nearly full bar, Tamara noticed some of the women. They looked busted. Tired-ass weaves, outdated clothes, and someone had the nerve to be wearing some white shoes.

"See what I mean," he said.

"Man, I know the sistahs can bring it better than this," Tamara said to the man who still hadn't introduced himself.

"Oh, don't get me wrong. There are some beautiful women here in H-town, but most of them are looking for the young thugs. You know, the ballers. I'm too old for that craziness," he said, bringing the Budweiser bottle to his pursed lips.

"Hmm, I see, so you hang out here and try to pick up those of us who are not really on our game?"

"Naw, that ain't even what I'm saying. All I'm trying to say is, I could tell you not a regular—that's all, baby girl. It's kinda like a compliment. You feel me?" he asked.

Tamara nodded. "Yeah, I feel you," she said.

"So what do you do here in Houston?" he asked.

"Actually, I'm from California. I'm about to relocate, so I was here looking at some houses."

"Oh, okay. Well, I just bought a house over in the 1960 Champions part of town. I like it over there. You know, it's a quiet, nice area."

"Did you build?" Tamara asked.

"Yeah, I did. What about you? What you looking at?"

"I just put something down on a nice place in the Royal Oaks area."

Tamara noticed his eyebrows go up. "That's that subdivision on the west side, right?" he asked.

"Yeah, I guess so."

He nodded and sipped his beer.

For the next couple of hours, Tamara and her new friend drank and danced a little. On their way back to the bar, she had to admit she was having a good time. Her decision to move to Houston was definitely a good one.

"You know, we've been chilling for the last few hours, drinking, talking, dancing, and having a good time, and I don't know your name," she finally said.

"I'm Donnell Jones," he said, pulling out the bar stool so she could take a seat. "And you, what's your name?"

"I'm Tamara Howard."

"Hmmm, Tamara, huh. I like that. So what do you do? I mean, you buying a house in Royal Oaks. I *know* you had to break off a nice piece of change for that," he said.

"Well, I'm about to open my own business. I'm opening a couple of full-service spas."

"You do hair?"

"Oh no, I'm not going to work in them. I'm going to manage them," she said.

"Damn, beauty and brains. That's tight," he said.

"Okay, enough about me. Whassup with you?"

"I've been working at a plant for about twenty years. I got my first job right out of high school, and just been doing my thang. I work for four days, then I'm off for four days. Since I've been at this spot for a minute, I got some seniority, so I work from six to six, and I'm straight. Nice salary—got myself a nice new house, a new F-150 truck, and I'm straight," he said.

Tamara looked at him as he spoke. He was a big man, tall, with a thick, muscular body to match. His light brown eyes offset his blackberry-colored skin. He wore a goatee, and his hair was in a smooth fade. He had on a pair of jeans and a pair of alligator boots. Everything about him was nice—a little country, as far as Tamara was concerned, but she liked him. A nice, big, corn-fed country bumpkin. She allowed her mind to venture into what he was working with, then shook off the dirty thought.

"Well, Donnell Jones, it's nice to meet you. I'm headed back to LA in the morning, but I'll be back to finish up with the house. I close in thirty days, and then I'm looking at a few sites for the salons."

Donnell used his left hand to stroke his goatee. "Say, sounds to me like you could use a friend here in the 'Bayou City.' You know, to help look out for your interests. I mean, on my days off, I wouldn't mind checking out a few spots for you. I could even help set up some meetings too," he suggested.

"You'd do that for me? I mean, you hardly even know me," she said.

"Yeah, but you seem like good peoples. 'Sides, you a sistah—a good-lookin' fine-ass sistah, I might add—trying to do something positive, so I'm down with that," he said.

Nikki looked at the money sitting in neat stacks on her coffee table. In the next four hours, she'd be seated at the blackjack table in "Sin City." And she couldn't wait. She kept looking at the clock. She wondered if there was any way she could shoot out to check up on Trey, but she knew she couldn't. She had already dropped off a basket at Marleeta's house for him. Marleeta wasn't there, but Nikki left it on the porch. She told herself staying around the apartment wouldn't do Trey or her any good. There was money to be made in Vegas, and she'd be damned if she didn't get her cut.

If she didn't want to save her money for the casino, she'd move her trip up, but she needed all the cash so she could multiply her money. Nikki struggled with the idea of how much money she should leave at the house. She had felt lucky before, but there was something different about how she felt this time. This time, she just knew she'd win. All she had to do was get to "Sin City," and get her gamble on.

When she couldn't stand it anymore, she said fuck it and decided to drive herself to the airport. Yeah, she'd be three hours early for the flight, but she didn't care. If she could, she'd try to catch an earlier flight. What the hell was she hanging around for anyway? She needed to strike while it was hot, and she felt lucky as hell.

Since she had to stop for gas, she decided to pass by the Normandie Casino, just to see if the parking lot was full. It wasn't. Nikki busted a quick U-turn and swung into the parking lot. She didn't even have to valet park, because there was a spot right next to the front door, reinforcing her lucky feeling.

"Hey, Ms. Lady, I hope you feeling lucky. They been paying out some serious cheddar up in here," the security guard said.

"Whhaaaat?" Nikki smiled. Another good sign.

The guard shook his head. "I was wondering where you been, I ain't seen you in a minute. I was like, dang, she straight missing out," he added.

"Well, I'm here now," she sang. Nikki wanted to run into the casino, she didn't feel like having small talk, but she didn't want to just blow the dude off. He was always nice to her.

When their conversation trailed off, Nikki couldn't make it through the doors fast enough. She was speed walking, and nearly ran over her favorite waitress. She didn't have time for more small talk, so she kept moving and claimed her spot at the blackjack table.

Two hours after she arrived, Nikki was on a fierce roll. She was up $15,000 and feeling fine. When the waitress came to drop off her fourth Pink Panty drink, Nikki tipped her $100.

"Thanks, Nikki. That's whassup," the waitress said as she kissed the chip and put it in her pocket.

"Just working my jelly. Gotta share the wealth." Nikki laughed before she told the dealer to hit her again.

Twenty-four hours after Nikki arrived at the Normandie Casino, she was still sitting tight in her chair at the blackjack table, and winning. Yeah, she had missed her flight to Vegas, but any true gambler knows you don't leave when the going is good. Nikki's ass was planted for as long as she was winning. *It's all gravy,* she told herself. Besides, she could always hop another bird to Vegas. For now, she was winning big, and she wasn't about to risk changing her luck. Shit, she'd stay a week if her luck allowed it.

The only time Nikki got up was to use the bathroom, and she often held it as long as she possibly could. One time she nearly pissed on herself right there, 'cause she didn't want to get up from her spot.

When she returned to the table, a light-skinned man, with a platinum grill and jewelry to match, smiled up at her. "Emm-hmm, Lady Luck just showed back up," he said toward Nikki.

She wasn't trying to hear what he was saying, though. She was on a roll, and she didn't need some busta trying to hang with a winner. Nikki knew the routine, everybody wants to be your friend when you winning big. Hell naw, she wasn't looking for any parasites. She didn't even return his bright-ass smile.

Sixteen hours later, Nikki wondered what the fuck had gone wrong. Ever since that wannabe rapper sat next to her, her pile of chips started dwindling. The shit was disappearing fast, and his stack was steadily growing.

"Hmm, guess you came and lucked up for real, huh?" She sneered in his direction. This time, she had to look around his new female friends, who had appeared out of nowhere.

"Oh, so now you can holla at a brotha, huh?" He snickered.

Nikki nodded and looked at him, then at her stack of chips neatly sitting in front of him.

"Just say the word and we can blow this joint," he said.

Nikki sucked her teeth, she'd get her win on again. She knew it, and she didn't need to go fuck no broke-down rapper, just 'cause he was on top momentarily. Shit, she'd get hers back.

Two hours after that, and $4,000 lighter, Nikki was hot. Dude was still winning and she was losing fast. She didn't know what to do or what to say. Feeling desperate and frustrated, she leaned over slightly, showing her cleavage.

"I see what you working with. Say, shorty, why don't you let me set you up this time," he offered.

Nikki couldn't refuse. When she looked down at the empty space in front of her, all she could do was smile at his offer. She was mad excited, but she wanted to play it cool.

"I 'preciate it, but I'm good for it," she said.

Twelve hours after the initial loan, Nikki had won $5,000. Unfortunately, she owed her new friend $20,000. Once again, the space in front of her, where stacks of chips once stood, was now empty. Nikki felt dejected, she was vexed, but she wanted again to try and maintain her composure.

When she looked over at her new friend, he stood. "Damn, girl, you did some real damage up in here. I ain't 'bout to sit here and lose all my money. 'Sides, I'm ready for you to pay up," he said.

Nikki frowned. "What?" she challenged, then looked around.

"Yeah, baby doll, a nigga ain't no bank and trust. Shit, I needs my snaps." Two men appeared at his side and collected his chips. "Y'all cash those in and we'll meet you outside," he said.

"We?" Nikki questioned as she threw him a cutting glare.

"Yeah, baby, you owe a nigga twenty grand. That ain't no chump change. So we 'bout to go get my money," he said.

Panic-stricken, Nikki widened her eyes in alarm. "Where the fuck am I supposed to get twenty thousand dollars from?" she asked.

"Now, I'd say that's your problem. But I'm sure if you think about it, you probably got at least one friend who can spot you the money," he offered.

"Huh, like hell I do. Naw, ain't nobody told your ass to be sitting up in here acting like big baller Bob. Shit, you go' have to wait. I'ma get you your money, but it's gonna take me a minute."

The man looked up at the camera in the ceiling and smiled at Nikki. "Here, why don't we move away from the table. We're done here. I need to holla at you for a minute," he said. He took her by the arm and started walking her toward the door.

Nikki didn't want to go anywhere with him. She started cursing at herself. Why didn't she just get on the fucking plane and go to Vegas? Shit, the only person she knew with that kind of money was Tamara. That is, if Tamara hadn't already blown her cash; otherwise, she'd have to ask Marleeta. And she didn't care what this fool threatened her with, she

would never do that. As she walked out of the
Normandie Casino with her new friend right at her
side, the guard looked up.

"Oh, dawg, I see you found her. I told you this her
spot—huh, Nikki?"

Sweet Revenge

Finding the female members of Marleeta's crew wasn't hard. When Nikki stopped by Marleeta's to drop off a basket, she had no idea she was being watched. She didn't have time to notice the black van sitting several houses down from Marleeta's driveway.

The guys took pictures and followed Nikki as she left Marleeta's house. It took no time to learn her weakness. She was a gambler. JD had told John to stay on her, but he also gave strict orders—making it clear that he didn't want any of the Headhunters hurt in any way whatsoever. Thanks to the surveillance they had on Marleeta's house, they knew she was in the midst of planning another job.

They also knew the guys were on vacation. Tamara was out of town, and Marleeta was busy setting up their next gig. JD said he wanted to make a move before the crew got together again. But he gave no sign of what he was planning to do. He told Richey Rich and John to get the information and bring it back to him.

When he felt he had enough information, he sent

his crew to the Normandie Casino. They showed the security guard Nikki's picture and paid him to call whenever she showed up. The guard insisted that if they waited around, she'd show up. But when he learned they were offering $500, he took the cash and promised he'd not only call, but he'd sit on her ass if he had to keep her there.

He had waited nearly a week to make that call. So the day he finally saw Nikki, he came up with the quick lie to make sure she'd stay until he was able to make the phone call.

JD's Hummer pulled up right in front of the Normandie Casino's doors as they opened and Nikki walked out with his boys at her side.

"Say, baby girl, whassup? Not your lucky night, huh?"

Nikki looked around the dark parking lot. Where the fuck was security when she needed them? She couldn't even try to make a dash for her car. Damn, she thought, until she saw JD sitting in the backseat.

"Aeey, what's going on?" She immediately felt better.

"Well, what's going on is, you owe my boy some serious cash, which means you owe me too. See, that was my money he was playing with, so that means you owe me."

Nikki's face broke into a wide grin. "Well, Daddy, why didn't he just say so? I don't mind owing you," she said. Nikki placed her hand on JD's thigh.

JD looked at the hand resting on his thigh: "Slow your roll," he said. "I need something from you and we can call it even," he said.

Nikki raised her eyebrow. She licked her lips and

stuck out her chest. "I'd be more than happy to work off my debt, baby." She sneered at the man who had loaned her the money. "As long as I get to work it off with you, Daddy."

"I got something else in mind," he said.

"Where to, JD?" the driver asked.

"Let's go back to the hotel. Then I want you guys to leave me alone with Nikki so we can talk and get our game plan together."

Hours later, Nikki enjoyed a steak dinner with JD. They were in a suite at the Four Seasons downtown.

"You didn't even have to go through all of this for me to help you get Marleeta. Shit, I can't stand that bitch. I woulda done this for free." She smiled.

"Is that right?" JD asked as he drank his cognac.

Nikki flinched. "A deal's a deal, though, right?"

"Oh yeah, you just do your part, like we agreed, and your slate is clean. I'm a man of my word," JD said.

"That's all I gotta do?" she asked.

"That's it," he said.

Nikki got up and sashayed a few feet from him. With her large ass facing JD, she turned her upper torso and put her hand on her hip. "You sure you don't want nothing else?" She cooed.

Let's Get Busy

Target: Roger Blake, aka Bling
Holdings: 200 million, in Lotto winnings
Estimated street net worth: ???
Drop schedule: every other Tuesday
Security detail: one driver and two motorcycles following behind
Weakness: women
Misc: loves kinky sex

When Roger Blake smiled for the cameras and held up his oversized Mega Millions check with so many zeros, Marleeta thought she was gonna come right there as she watched the TV screen. But she didn't—instead, she immediately went to work, learning as much about him as she could.

Three weeks after their break, the Headhunters were ready to go back to work. This would be the first job since Trey was back home. He wasn't in the lineup, but he was going to be all right. The crew agreed to give him a cut, even though he would be on the sidelines.

Zack had gotten the call five days after he and Danny Boy had returned from their trip. Trey had called, saying bring the wire cutters, he was ready to bust outta there, and they were more than ready to make it happen. At two in the morning, Zack and Danny Boy went and picked him up. They cut the handcuffs from his arm and pulled him outta the room before the nurses could hit the security button.

Tamara and Nikki were rolling together, since this target wanted to fuck two females at the same time. Tamara had been sent in to work him, after Marleeta had found a sex tape of him on the Internet. Tamara made it clear she was down for whatever, and he wanted to make sure she meant it.

Bling would've never come under the Headhunter radar, had he not been arrested and accused of financing a Fresno drug dealer's last stash. It seems the news media found out Roger Blake was none other than the sole winner of the multistate Mega Millions Lotto in Louisiana. When he won the money, he relocated to California to escape greedy friends and family members.

Of course he bonded out of jail right away. When Marleeta read up on him, she knew she had to change plans and make him a priority. She had booked a room at the Hotel Californian, and they were set up and ready for business. They had been working him for two weeks. The fool was flashy and spent money like it was going out of style.

The ladies got hot and bothered just thinking about him and taking his money. When Tamara finally got to his house, it took her about two days to learn of his little fantasy. It was on and poppin', since she had already peeped his operation and learned he had tons of cash on hand. The fucker was guilty of the charges, but before he went back to jail, the Headhunters planned on making his pockets a little lighter.

When they pulled the rental car up at his house on Clinton Avenue, Nikki found herself getting all excited too. This job would be her chance to get paid, and stack her bank back up. Yeah, she and JD had a deal, but outside of what he was talking about, she needed to make some money.

"You ready for this?" Tamara asked.

"Shit, I stays ready, 'specially when cash is involved," Nikki said.

They walked up to Bling's door and knocked softly. When he opened the door, the first thing Nikki noticed was his developing potbelly. He wasn't quite what she was expecting, but she had to do what she had to do.

"Girls, am I glad to see you. I thought you got lost or something." He smiled.

Bling was actually wearing a cigar coat and matching house shoes. He wasn't ugly, but he just wasn't fine either.

"Daddy, you know I would've called if we couldn't find you," Tamara cooed. "This is my girl I told you about. They call her Nasty Nancy."

Bling reached out and grabbed Nikki's ass.

"Damn, Carla, I think we got a real live one here," Nikki joked. She shook her ass as she walked into the house.

Bling clapped his hands and music flooded the room. The lights had already been dimmed. There was an array of liquor lining the coffee table.

"*Ooooh,* and he got taste too," Nikki said as she bounced toward the liquor.

"Girl, I told you, Bling do things big—real big—huh, Daddy?" Tamara batted her eyes and smiled.

Bling lay back on his leather sofa and lifted his legs to the coffee table. "So lookie here. Why don't y'all pull off them jackets so I could see what we working with up in here."

"Before we get to that, we got a surprise for you," Tamara said.

Tamara stood near the table and started swaying to the music. A few seconds later, Nikki came up and started to help her undress. Bling was beside himself. Once Tamara had stripped down to her matching bra and thong set, she rubbed her fingers up and down her body.

"Yeah, baby, that's what I'm sayin'. Work it for Daddy, baby," Bling cried out as he sucked his liquor through a straw.

When Tamara finished her solo performance, she helped Nikki get out of her clothes. The minute she was down to her thong and bra, Bling dramatically clutched his chest as if he were suffering an attack.

Upon seeing this, Nikki worked her big ass closer to his face and lingered there until she felt his palms and his lips up against her ass cheeks.

"*Daaaaayuuum.* Y'all 'bout to send a nigga to an early grave. Carla, how you know I was an ass man?"

Tamara acted like she was hurt. She pouted. "But, Daddy, I thought you said you liked my titties." She rubbed her nipples through the lace.

"Oh shit, girl, you putting a serious hurting on me," he cried. "You know I loves me some titties too. 'Specially the nice set you gots there," he said.

Bling started stroking his shaft. "*Sssssssssssss,* lemme see y'all kiss," he said.

Before he could settle down, Tamara opened her mouth and stuck out her tongue. Nikki dramatically licked it, then sucked it.

"*Ooooooh . . . damn.* I done died and gone to heaven. *Daaaayuuum!*" Bling squealed.

Still stroking himself, with his eyes glued to the two women, he could barely sit still.

Nikki reached up and squeezed Tamara's breast. When she did, Tamara released a hearty moan, which seemed to drive Bling wild.

"Oh shit," he cried. He started stroking himself, faster and harder. "Yeah, Nancy, I wanna see that ass of yours," he said.

Tamara helped Nikki by pulling down her thong. When she did, she rubbed Nikki's ass slowly, and ran her body up against her back and bare behind.

"C'mon over here," Bling said.

They walked over, and Bling slid off the couch and onto the floor. The minute his head hit the floor, Nikki sat on his face. She started gyrating her hips slowly, helping to work her body into a comfortable position. He grabbed her ass and started squeezing. Not to be outdone, Tamara started stroking his dick. It wasn't massive, but she could work with it.

"You having a good time, Daddy?"

Unable to speak, Bling tapped his foot three times and squeezed Nikki's ass even harder.

The dick started looking good to Tamara. She started thinking about Donnell and that thick-ass body of his. She reached into her jacket pocket and pulled out a condom. Before Bling could catch his breath, she slid it on and flopped herself onto his stiff dick.

"Aaaaaahhhhhh," Tamara cried. With her back to Nikki's back, she rode Bling's dick until she felt her juices sliding down his shaft.

When Nikki felt that tickling sensation in the bottom of her feet, she clinched her thighs together like a vise grip and held Bling's head in place. *"Yesssss,* right there! Right there, Daddy, right there!" By now, Bling had a firm grip on her breasts and was ready to explode himself.

As he was about to explode, he bit Nikki's clit between his teeth, sending her into a fury. When she collapsed on her side, Bling's entire face was covered in her juices. Tamara turned around and rode him as he squeezed her nipples till they burned. Just as they were about to come together, the front door crashed to the floor.

Nikki screamed and scrambled for cover. Tamara tumbled off Bling and scurried toward her clothes on the floor. Bling looked around, like he wasn't sure what was going on.

"Stay your big ass right there, or this bullet is going straight for that little dick you got," the gunman said. He looked around the room. "This can go real smooth. Get your big ass up and lead us to the safe," he added.

Bling closed his eyes. "Don't shoot, man. You can have whatever you want. Just don't shoot."

On the Road Again

The drive back to LA was only expected to take four or five hours. Zack and Marleeta left as soon as the sun came up, the other three were set to fly out later in the afternoon. The crew planned to meet up at Marleeta's house later that night.

Neither Zack nor Marleeta spoke for the first hour of the road trip. But when he hit the grapevine—a winding mountainous part of the route between Bakersfield and Los Angeles—Zack looked over at her.

"You know you should've come to the Keys with me," he said.

"And why's that?"

"Shit, you would've had a blast. A nigga like myself was well rested when I got back. That was the shit," Zack said.

"*Emph,* who you take? Some chickenhead I'm sure," Marleeta said.

Zack chuckled. "Why she gotta be a chickenhead?"

"Oh, my bad, a hoodrat then." Marleeta had to laugh at her own petty jealousy. She had no idea why it bothered her to know Zack took some other female to the Keys. Shit, did she expect him to go alone? She wondered whether he put his tongue on her clit and rubbed it up and down.

"Why you hating? You know I wanted to take you, but, shit, you be treating a nigga like he a straight scrub. You'll recognize soon enough." He huffed. "Keep waiting on them niggas like JD with his tired ass. I told you, you need to give this young buck a shot. I know how to handle mines, you best believe it," he said.

Marleeta wondered if she would have to listen to Zack go on about himself for the remainder of the ride.

"You see the way you all wound up, all tight? That's 'cause you ain't got no man, baby. You know, somebody to help ease your mind and help you relax. I don't know what kinda fools you kicking it with, but my woman would be running around with a big-ass smile plastered on her face. And a nigga like me would work hard to make sure it stays there."

"Yeah, yeah yeah, you just bumpin' your gums. All of y'all wanna talk about what you would do, and how you'd hold it down, and how you could keep a bitch satisfied, and shit. But then things get old and you start sniffing around for new tail."

"*Whhhaaaat?* Damn, Queenie, somebody done did a number on you. I ain't even like the average nigga, baby. I'm about mines. Yeah, I handle my business inside the bedroom and out. Fo'sheezy," he said. "I know you think a nigga all young and not worldly enough for you, but you got that all wrong. See, I'm about doing some things. You think I wanna be in the stickup game forever—hell naw . . . but I'm taking my money and making investments. When I was in the Keys, shit, I was looking at some investment properties. I got my uncle who's gonna front my shit. We 'bout to close on some shit in the Cayman Islands in a few weeks."

Marleeta's eyebrow shot upward. She was surprised. She didn't expect this little boy to actually be planning for the future. The more she thought about Zack, he wasn't like Trey or Danny Boy. They both wore their money on their wrists, chests, and in their ears. Not Zack. He always looked neat and clean, dressed somewhat trendy, but not too over the top.

He wore one sports watch and a diamond stud in his ear—that was it. Zack was never iced out. Since Marleeta paid him, she knew he had money, but he didn't walk around frozen, screaming about his wealth. The other two were the opposite. They basically walked around looking like rap stars.

"Yeah, I'm making my money work for me. You think a nigga wanna be in his thirties or forties doing this shit? Hell naw, I'ma take care of mines now, so I can have something later and stay off these damn streets."

Marleeta felt herself nodding at his logic. "That's smart, Zack, I had no idea," she confessed.

"See, that's what I'm talking about. There's a lot you don't know about a nigga. You look at me and think I'm like the rest of these young bucks running around. It ain't so, baby, not hardly. I'm a nigga with a plan. All I need is my Bonnie by my side, a real ride-or-die chick." Zack chuckled. "I'm saying, Marleeta, why don't you let a nigga tighten you up a bit."

Marleeta shook her head. "You tripping, Zack.

What am I supposed to do? Let you hit it, then we just go back to business as usual? You know it don't work like that," she said.

"Look, boss lady, you running this shit, right?"

"Right," Marleeta confirmed.

"You think you 'bout to let anybody or anything prevent you from making that cheddar? That ain't even like you. That's what I like about you, baby. You all about the business. I'm just saying, we could make one helluva team. That's why I wanted to take you to Key West."

"What, so you could lick my clit?" She laughed.

"See you got jokes. But that's a'ight. Baby, everybody needs some release and relaxation. That's all I'm saying. I think you should think about us before you just count a nigga out. You should at least give me a try. We could keep it on the down low, you know, so it don't affect business."

Before she could stop herself, Marleeta said, "Okay, what the hell."

Zack swerved and nearly drove them off the road. "For real, Queenie?"

Marleeta shook her head. On the inside, she was all smiles.

"I'm sayin' just try me," he said.

Pay Up

JD was sick and tired of his partnership with Nikki already. He hadn't heard from her in days, and suspected she was working another job. This was after he thought he had an understanding with her. Until she fulfilled her part of their agreement, she still owed him—and he owned that ass.

It had been nearly a month since he and Nikki decided how to deal with Marleeta. JD couldn't believe he fell for her game. Yeah, his boys had said she was a cold piece, but still something about her intrigued him. Since he realized he had been got, he couldn't keep his mind off her. Her little hustle was rather tight too. No, he didn't like being taken for a fool, but, shit, he had to admit her shit was tight.

Damn, he straight had plans for her too. JD was used to women throwin' it at him. That had been happening since his street days, the times when he was hugging the corners so tight a bitch couldn't help but wanna be on his team. But in recent years, he had gotten careful. He wasn't just out there like he was before. JD and his boys may have partied with women, but JD was very careful about who he took back to his place.

He let his guard down with Marleeta, 'cause he thought she was the one. The way she stepped to him—yeah, he had seen her, even heard about her crew—but he had no idea they were in the stickup game. JD started wondering just how many other niggas had fallen victim to their little game.

With so much time on his hands, his brain was working, and he had to truly admit to himself, what he felt for Marleeta went far beyond admiration for what she was able to pull off. She haunted his sleep at night. When he woke, she was the very first thought that entered his mind. He found himself going over every little detail so that he could remember how she looked, what she wore, and even how she walked.

JD picked up the cell phone and dialed Nikki's number. When she answered, he had to take a deep breath.

"Yo, whassup? I know you didn't forget about me."

"Ooh, naw, baby. You know I could never do that."

JD waited, but Nikki didn't say anything else. He heard slot machines in the background.

"So whassup with the business we got together?"

"Oh, Daddy, you know I ain't forgot. We just got back from a job yesterday, but I'm working on it. You said yourself it would take some time. Don't trip—I got you, I got you. Yeah, hit me again," she said.

"Look, I ain't got all fucking day. You need to handle the business, and stay the fuck outta them casinos. That's what got your ass in the situation you in now," he screamed.

"Say, JD, you ain't got to talk to me like that. Me

being in the casino ain't really none of your business. I told you already, I'ma take care of what we agreed to, but I ain't gonna have you sweating me all hard like this. 'Cause I could come over there and drop off your fucking money and go about my business—you feel me?"

JD was hot. "Word? Who the fuck do you think you talking to like that? I'm not one of these punk-ass niggas you used to—" He suddenly stopped talking. JD inhaled, then exhaled.

"Look, man, why you tripping? We got this. I done already told you, it's gonna be my pleasure to help you bring that bitch down."

"I don't think you understand," JD said. "*You* work for me! And I think you got me all twisted. But that's okay, I ain't gonna talk about it, I'ma be about it. Believe that." JD hung up. He dialed John and barked instructions through gritted teeth.

Marleeta and Zack had been in bed for two whole days. He went from sucking her pussy to thrashing it in delicious ways she never knew possible. *Damn, this young nigga got me all sprung and shit, already!* The way he worked his hips and his lips kept her wanting more and more. When he told her he had some business to tend to, she didn't even want him to go, for fear something might happen to prevent him from coming back.

"C'mon, girl, you know I'm coming back. I just need to go check up on Trey, make sure he gets paid and shit." Zack massaged her bare breast, sending raw heat running all through her body.

If she had it her way, they'd spend another two days in bed, wrapped up in each other's body parts and fucking at will.

"Okay, but don't make me come looking for you," she warned.

"Boo, you got me. And that's on the real. A nigga ain't gonna lose his way home—shit, not when he got you waiting on him."

After he left, Marleeta locked her door and walked back to the bedroom. She jumped onto the bed and closed her eyes. She wanted to relive each scrumptious second of the incredible pleasure her body had experienced over the last forty-eight hours.

After she had agreed to give it—*them*—a try, Zack damn near raced back to the house. A couple of times she had to remind him to slow down. They were, of course, transporting tons of cash, and neither wanted to have to explain to five-o where the fuck they got all that money.

He agreed, but she had to warn him again later.

"I'm sorry, babe. I just wanna hurry up and get you to the house. I got something for you."

"And I want it too, Zack, but, shit, we got business to tend to at the house, remember? Everybody still gotta get paid," she reminded him.

"Yeah, but if we get there early, I could give you a sample of what's to come. The crew ain't coming in till later tonight anyway," he said.

"True that, true that."

Zack put the pedal to the metal and made it back to Marleeta's in record time. Once he pulled the bags of cash out of the vehicle, he pulled her inside. He attacked her passionately the minute they closed the door.

But Marleeta's passion was just as fierce as his. For every pull and tuck he made toward her clothes, she matched, by attacking his.

"Oh shit, girl, you got a nigga all in heat." He was huffing and puffing.

"I want it," Marleeta cooed.

They didn't even make it to the sofa. Right there, on the floor, at the door, they stripped each other's clothes off. Zack opened her legs, tossed them over his shoulders, and used the tips of his fingers to separate the lips of her pussy.

Marleeta scratched and crawled at his flesh. She had done this so many times in her dreams, she wanted this reality to last forever.

Zack used his moist tongue and licked her from the hood, which covered her clit, to the opening of her pussy.

She yelped as he adjusted himself, then her legs, which were draped over his shoulders. He had her wide open. Just when she thought she was experiencing a high, she felt what she had only experienced through his words and her imagination.

Zack's tongue sat on her clit for a few seconds. She felt herself going wild. She wanted to scream, tighten her thighs around his head, and dig her nails deep into his flesh.

After a few seconds, his tongue started moving up and down, up and down.

Marleeta released a screeching howl. Still, Zack's tongue rubbed.

"Ooooooooooooh, my God!"

Zack's tongue sat and rubbed, picking up momentum, and it slid up and down her clit.

Marleeta was losing her fucking mind. Could this be real? Was she finally feeling what she had dreamt about for hours on end? Was this the very best pussy eater alive? She couldn't stand it anymore! It was too good; it felt way too good. Too much pleasure. Marleeta fought to push his head away, but still he rubbed.

She shoved with all of her might, but he didn't budge. His tongue simply rubbed up and down. When she thought she'd absolutely die from so much—too much—pleasure, the soles of her feet started burning. Then they tingled, and she wanted—no, needed—help.

But Zack's tongue still rubbed, like it had a mind of its own. Like it was obsessed and determined.

Marleeta started trying to scoot back on her ass. But Zack and his tongue moved with every inch she managed.

"Ooooh God. Oh, Zack! Oh shit!" she cried. Still, his tongue rubbed. He added a little more pressure and she squealed.

"Zzzzzzack!" she hollered. "I'm . . . um. I'm commming," she sobbed.

When Zack felt her juices erupt, he quickly sopped them up and sucked her opening. Before he got up, he kissed her lips, her thighs, and her belly button.

He looked down at the smile plastered across her face and considered his job well done.

That evening, everyone got paid the minute they stepped through the doors. Marleeta was very pleasant, but she let it be known she had plans. Zack even left, as if he hadn't just sent her to cloud nine and back. After Nikki got her money and left, he returned for round two.

Just when Marleeta thought things couldn't get any better, Zack unveiled his fabulous, massive dick.

That's when she knew for sure she was in heaven and he was a keeper.

Tamara and Donnell had been talking on the phone every day since she returned to LA. He already had three properties for her to look at during her next trip to Houston. He also told her he would help her move. He said there was no need for her to spend thousands of dollars, when he could do it during his days off.

After speaking to him for the second time one particular day, she was glad she didn't just leave him at the bar. His help had proven quite valuable already. They agreed to take things slow. He didn't mind being called a friend, but he did let her know his long-term intentions included making her his woman.

Tamara was about to leave for a trip to her safe-deposit box when her phone rang. She looked at the caller ID and considered not answering, but she didn't want Nikki showing up at her door.

"Hey, girly, whassup?" Nikki asked the second Tamara said hello.

"Just headed out the door. What's going on with you?"

"Not a damn thing. I was calling to see if you wanted to come with me to the Normandie. You know, they have a big ole party on Saturday nights. I

thought maybe we could find ourselves a man."
Nikki chuckled at her invite.

"Oh naw, girl, I ain't looking for no damn man.
And you know how I feel 'bout gambling. I work too
hard for my money to go feed it to some damn slot
machine," Tamara said.

"Girl, I don't waste my time on those slots either.
I'm into blackjack. Shit, I won twenty Gs yesterday!"
Nikki bragged.

"*Whaaat?* Really?" Tamara faked interest.

"Uh-huh. Girl, I'm always winning up in that bitch.
Why you think I stay up in there?" Nikki said.

"Well, thanks for calling me, but, girl, I got too much
shit to take care of," Tamara said. "I need to run."

"Oh, okay. Well, I was just checking to see if you
wanted to go. If you change your mind, you know
where to find me."

"Cool. Have fun," Tamara said as she rolled her
eyes and pushed the end button on her cell phone.

What the hell would she look like going to a damn
casino? Nikki had a fucking gambling problem, as
far as Tamara was concerned. Look at where she
lived, on the bottom. Ain't no way in the world somebody making as much as she made should be living
like that.

Tamara thought about the last time she went to
Nikki's apartment. She couldn't believe it when they
pulled up in front of the raggedy-ass building.
Tamara sat there for a moment, afraid Nikki would
ask her to come inside.

When she stepped into the matchbox of an apartment, there was an odor that threatened to slam her into the wall. Tamara looked around the small, dark room.

"You don't smell that?" she asked Nikki.

"What, girl?"

"That! Damn, you need to open up a window in here. How come you don't smell that?"

"Oh, girl, I'm used to it. My toilet is broken. And these motherfucka's don't fix shit around this camp," Nikki said. "We only gon' be here for a hot minute. Lemme grab my shit and we out."

Tamara watched as Nikki rambled through a closet, which looked like it was full of junk. She pulled a few clothes from a pile on the floor and ran toward the kitchen. Tamara stayed at the door.

There was a small partition that separated her bed from the living-room area. After a few minutes, Tamara opened the door and stepped outside. She couldn't believe Nikki lived like that.

"Hmm, that's her fucking problem," Tamara mumbled as she locked her door and headed to the bank.

She wanted to put the envelopes stuffed with cash into her safe-deposit box, then go have lunch to review the information Donnell had sent. Tamara decided she was going to get out of the game in six months. If she had to, she could pull it off now, but six months would be enough time for her, and everybody else, to stack some extra cash. She told herself, everything from here on out would be gravy. She already had the meat and potatoes, but gravy would be nice.

The Heat
Is On

Nikki trembled as the tears ran down her cheeks. It's not supposed to go down like this. Fuck, nobody would even miss her ass, or report her missing. What the fuck was she going to do? When she heard footsteps and voices in the other room, fear gripped her heart. Her breathing quickened and the bottom of her stomach fell. She didn't know how long she had been locked in the room. She was blindfolded, and her hands were tied at her back.

She would've screamed long ago, but the tape across her mouth prevented that too. She knew her greed would eventually get the best of her, but never did she think it would happen like this.

Nikki's lucky streak started running out after she was up close to $50,000. She told herself to leave with the cash. Just take it and run, but the more she won, the more she wanted more. It wasn't until she had lost damn near every penny that she got up and sulked out of the casino.

They had come out of nowhere. She was tearing up the trunk of her car, hoping she might've dropped a one-hundred-dollar bill and didn't know it. But the trunk, full of junk, had no cash lying around in it. Nikki sucked her teeth and was prepared to shut it, when she was grabbed from behind.

"Bitch, shut the fuck up, or I'll snap your neck right here!" the voice warned.

Nikki's heart was racing so fast, she thought it would leap from her chest. She tried to think calm thoughts. But, shit, here she was broke again, and being kidnapped to boot. What the fuck happened to her lucky streak? She didn't even try to fight the man who threatened to end her life. She allowed her body to collapse into his arms and closed her eyes.

She prayed they wouldn't kill her, but then decided it wouldn't be all that bad if they didn't torture her first. That had been hours ago. Nikki only knew that, because while she sat tied to a chair and blindfolded, she had pissed on herself twice and her stomach was growling. Her record for holding her piss at the blackjack table had been four hours. By her estimation, she had been held for at least eight hours, and no less than six.

If only she knew what it was that she had done, who was out to get her? Maybe it was one of the targets who had finally figured out their hustle. But wouldn't they be after Marleeta? Shit, Nikki wasn't the mastermind behind the Headhunters. The minute they removed the tape, she'd start singing. She'd tell them that she wasn't the one in charge. The Queen Bee was Marleeta, that's who they wanted. That's who should be sitting taped to a fucking chair and blindfolded, not her!

Nikki had decided she'd rat them all out if it meant saving her ass. But she wouldn't give up all the information right away. No, she'd lure them with a little, then demand her release and some cash before she gave up the rest of them.

She felt no loyalty to anyone. Look at how Tamara had treated her when she called her. Then there was Marleeta's ass always looking down her nose, like she was better than everybody. She still felt bad about Trey—but truth be told, if her ass was on the line, she'd toss his ass to the lions too. Make no doubt about it: she was not about to go down alone, and certainly not for Marleeta.

Her train of thought was interrupted when she heard the door swing open. She immediately started squirming in her chair.

"Mmmmmmm," she mumbled.

When she heard the familiar voice, sadly, everything suddenly fell into place.

Marleeta was in heaven. Her young dick was the lick and she felt on top of the world. She couldn't get enough of Zack, every time she saw him her panties got wet. And he was right there to sop up her juices. As they lay in bed, after yet another marathon sex session, she thought of how she almost allowed something so magnificent to slip through her fingers. Well, she was glad she finally woke up and opened up to accept all he had to offer.

The game now was keeping their relationship a

secret. Zack promised he wouldn't say anything, because he understood what it could do with the crew. Marleeta hoped he truly understood why she didn't want her business all out in the streets. There were a couple of things she wanted to get her fingers on so they could ride into the retirement sunset with their pockets full and no loose ends.

"When are we going back to work?" Zack asked as he rolled onto his back.

"I'm working on something. I should know for sure by the middle of next week," Marleeta assured him.

"Oh, okay, cool. Well, I need to run to the Valley for a coupla days," Zack said. Before Marleeta could ask any questions, he got up and made his way to the bathroom. He was a sight to see, her eyes zeroed in on his thick ass. His muscular legs and back were incredible. She still couldn't get over how big his trunk of a dick was. It was thick, dark, and long. Lately she had been thinking about how she would simply walk away from what was definitely the best sex of her entire life. Imagine, the same young buck she dismissed months ago now had her climbing the walls daily.

After she heard the water go on, Marleeta went into the bathroom. Through the steam, she could see her man-child lathering his body with soap. She liked everything about Zack, his laid-back style, his rock-hard body, and the way he aimed to please her—no matter what it took. She hoped they'd always be that way.

The minute she stepped into the shower, he turned and started lathering her body with soap. His calloused hands rubbed her breasts, her stomach, thighs, and gripped her ass. Just his touch alone was able to ignite deep sexual sparks in her.

After Zack left, Marleeta went to the computer. She started going over the jobs she had to abandon when they decided to move on Bling instead. By her calculations, she would be ready to get out in another six months. During that time, she hoped to complete a total of five jobs. Marleeta didn't want to get careless or greedy during her last months on the grind, but she wanted to make sure each job was well worth their time and effort.

They were discussing whether they should revisit the target they had to abandon when Trey got shot. Tamara had put in work with him and never had the chance to see the results of her labor. Marleeta decided to put him on the back burner, since he was so close to home.

A week later, the Headhunters were in Miami. Marleeta had booked a room at the trendy Sagamore, the Art Hotel, on Collins Avenue.

"Damn, Queenie, we doing big thangs ourselves," Tamara commented as they stepped out of the Lincoln Town Car in front of the hotel's lobby.

"Yeah, I feel special, the way the place is all lit up and shit. And these palm trees," Nikki said.

Their suite was on the sixth floor and it was laid. Nikki and Tamara were impressed.

"Okay, let's settle down, then head out to the club," Marleeta said.

"Where we going tonight?" Tamara asked.

"B.E.D.," Marleeta tossed over her shoulder as she walked into her room.

"That club they showed on that *CSI* episode? The one with all the beds? People ate, drank, and basically just chilled out on beds. It was a trip."

"Yeah, that's the one," Marleeta hollered from her room.

"Damn, how we getting up in there?" Tamara mumbled. When she looked up, Marleeta was standing in the doorway.

"That's what you guys got me for. You don't have to worry about stuff like that. I got us covered," she said.

A few hours later, the three were dressed and ready to go. Marleeta called the front desk and asked them to ring her room when the car service arrived. Marleeta had on a skintight Calvin Klein copper-colored slip dress, with matching heels and a clutch purse. Her skin glowed. Her hair was pulled up in a bun on top of her head, with curls hanging in the back and near her temple.

Tamara wore a pair of white low-rise jeans, with a tube top, and her hair in spiral curls. When Nikki stepped out in her black lace boy shorts and matching tank top, with a lace robe, Marleeta and Tamara exchanged knowing looks.

"Damn, girl, you going to bed or you going out?" Tamara joked.

"Well, let y'all tell it, I'm doing both, right? So I figure I might as well dress the part." Nikki looked like she was getting ready to star in a soft-core porn flick. On a normal body, the outfit would've been somewhat tasteful. With her oversized behind, it just looked X-rated.

"You don't think you should put on some jeans or something?" Marleeta asked before she thought better of it.

"Why you hating, Queenie? Y'all just mad 'cause you know I'm 'bout to have all the niggas jocking," she said.

Marleeta nodded her head and said fuck it. "Okay, the car should be here in twenty minutes." She passed pictures to Nikki, then Tamara. "These are our targets. We got two weeks to make something happen, 'cause I'd like to move on them in a week, so we can pull up outta here."

Nikki and Tamara studied their pictures. As usual, Nikki thought, she got the one with the face of a bulldog, some nigga named "Colt," while Tamara's target, Kenny "Fly" Brown, looked good. She sucked her teeth and glanced at the mug shot again. As they got on the elevator, Nikki looked at Marleeta and asked, "So when is Zack and the boys coming in?"

"Why you asking me about Zack?" Marleeta said with too much attitude.

Nikki's head snapped back. She looked at Tamara, who looked at Marleeta, with a frown on her face.

"Ah, I was just wondering when they were coming in town. What's the big deal?"

Marleeta caught herself, and quickly said, "The boys will be here at the end of the week."

As they stepped out of the hotel and into the humid Miami night, Nikki rolled her eyes at Marleeta the second she turned her back.

They were outside for about two minutes when

the car pulled up. They hopped in and rode silently to the club.

On the ride over to club B.E.D., Nikki kept thinking about her last run-in with JD and his boys. It had been a scare tactic that worked. She now knew he meant business. What she didn't understand was why he was so fucking obsessed with Marleeta's skinny ass.

JD basically tossed her to the side, once he got what he wanted. She was hoping her pussy would be her ticket to locking him down, but even after she fucked him something fierce, he still had the nerve to be all caught up on Marleeta. Nikki didn't know what niggas saw in her skinny ass.

Yeah, JD had one of his punk-ass boys rough her up a bit, but what he didn't know was the minute he got a call and had to rush out, she had John eating out of the palm of her hand. Nikki was always able to spot the ass man in the crew.

John got one whiff of her almighty booty and he was all about willing to settle her debt with JD his damn self. John was a cool fuck too, but she wanted JD. So when he told her to call him from their next job, she agreed. She even told him she didn't mean to sound so nonchalant the last time they spoke. She blamed it on the gambling, saying sometimes she got too excited while on her streak. He said he understood, but he warned her not to let it happen again.

When the phone hung up, she had no idea he'd send his boys to scoop her up from the Normandie Casino, but that's exactly what he did. They didn't

even have to do her like that, but it was okay, though.
Nikki couldn't wait to see the look on Marleeta's face
when JD finally executed his revenge. She wanted to
make sure she'd be right by his side. She also wanted
to make sure Marleeta knew she had a hand in the
process. *Oooooh,* she couldn't stand Marleeta. But
Nikki had to admit, she did like the way Marleeta
handled business.

The line to enter B.E.D. was wrapped around the
corner. But their car pulled up out front, the driver
got out, opened their door and the bouncer removed
the velvet rope and allowed the three of them to walk
right in.

"Sweet Saturdays" at B.E.D. was a gathering of the
exotically beautiful people in South Beach, Miami. The
crowd consisted mainly of model-looking women,
video hoes, athletes, and rapper-type men. Everywhere
Nikki stepped, men's eyes lingered and women started
whispering and twisting up their faces. But she didn't
care, she knew she was the shit.

Marleeta's instructions were clear. They were to
separate and search for their targets. They'd meet in
the ladies' room two hours after they arrived to com-
pare notes; then they'd meet every two hours after,
until somebody came up.

Nikki could tell from all the play she was getting,
she'd probably be going home with her target. She
walked over to a pink bedroom with a round bed, surrounded by palm trees, with pink sheer dividers.
When the other females saw all that ass she was
packing, they got up and walked to another part of

the club. *Smart girls,* Nikki thought. *I know they don't want none.*

By the time Nikki got comfortable on the bed, a waitress came over to inform her two drinks were available for her enjoyment. She ordered a glass of Hypnotiq, and the next time the waitress came, she brought the bottle.

"This is compliments of the gentleman over there," she said.

Nikki smiled and looked in the direction the waitress had pointed. She'd be damned if it wasn't Tamara's target! He nodded his head when their eyes met and held up his glass.

A few minutes later, he strolled over to the bed Nikki was on and asked if he could join her.

"Yeah, but I need to run to the little girl's room. You promise to keep my spot warm?" she asked.

"Baby, with an ass like that, I'll do anything you want." He smiled.

Nikki gave him a special treat and shook her ass extra hard as she sashayed to the ladies' room. Marleeta and Tamara were already in there when she arrived. "Say, I think we got a problem. I just met Kenny Brown."

Tamara shrugged. "Work it, girlfriend."

"You don't mind?" Nikki asked.

"Why would she? This is business, remember? Whatever it takes to get the job done. Do your thang," Marleeta said.

And Nikki intended to. The minute they left her behind in the bathroom, she pulled her cell phone from her purse and called JD.

"Where you staying?" she asked.

"Don't worry about that. Just know I'm here. Where y'all at?"

"B.E.D.," she said.

"On Washington? I know exactly where it's at. Good looking-out," he said.

"Anything for you, Daddy," she cooed.

"Yo, save that shit, Nikki. I'll holla," he said.

Nikki was pissed about JD. She knew he only wanted to get to Marleeta, and she wasn't happy about it, but since she owed him, she had to do what he wanted. Nikki was hoping she'd be around to see Marleeta's face when she spotted JD here in Miami's South Beach.

But for now, she had business to tend to. She was about to get to know Mr. Brown better and figure out if he knew what to do with all the ass she had.

Nikki added more lipstick, powdered her face, then turned to see what her ass looked like in the lace shorts she was wearing. She pulled them out of her crack, then adjusted the padding in her push-up bra top, and walked out of the ladies' room.

When Nikki returned to the pink bed, there was an oval-shaped tray with drinks and appetizers. The 50 Cent song "Just a Lil' Bit" flowed through the speakers and she started moving her hips to the beat. When she turned around to face Kenny and shake her ass just a little bit, several men suddenly appeared.

"Back off, she's mine," Kenny pretended to yell. Nikki looked at the small group of guys and reconfirmed what she had known for a long time. Tons of men prefer a big ass, no matter what it's attached to.

Nikki laid her hands flat on the bed, then swung her leg over and seductively crawled onto the bed.

She slid her body next to Kenny's and cuddled as close to him as possible. He used his hands to palm her ass. "Damn, girl, you 'bout to start all kinds of shit up in here. I know you coming home with me tonight, right?"

Tamara wasn't jealous, but she was damn near bored. Nikki's original target still hadn't made an appearance at the club, and Marleeta wasn't the best company. So while Nikki was damn near fucking Tamara's target, Kenny "Fly" Brown, Tamara was stuck on a blue bed with Marleeta, who sat with a cell phone glued to her ear. Tamara had no idea who she was giggling and whispering with on the phone, but the shit was working her nerves.

The club was tight, no doubt, but Tamara wanted to get to work, so they could hit the road and get back to LA. Donnell was going to visit and she couldn't wait to see him. Tamara looked up and noticed it was time for them to meet in the ladies' room again. She started to interrupt Marleeta's phone sex, then thought better of it and hopped off the bed.

She sashayed toward the ladies' room, scanning all of the beds she passed. She didn't see anyone who looked like Colt. Honestly, she couldn't help feeling like she should've been where Nikki was. But compared to Nikki and most of the women in the club, she and Marleeta looked like they were dressed for church rather than a trendy nightclub made up of beds.

Tamara waited a few minutes before Nikki came strolling in.

"Whassuuup?" Nikki giggled. She bent over and looked beneath the row of stalls. "Where the fuck is Queenie?"

"Girl, she out there blowing sweet nothings to somebody over the phone." Tamara sucked her teeth.

"Guuuurl, you see how she flashed on me when I asked about the boys? I'm telling you, Tamara, she unstable. I'm telling you, we need to smooth do our own thing. And what's this shit with your target, um, I mean my target. Well, my original target, that nigga Colt, girl, he look like somebody's toilet. Just nasty," Nikki said as she adjusted her shorts.

"Yeah, he is pretty booty. But, girl, be glad you ain't got to deal with his ass," Tamara offered.

"Hmm, girl, don't look like you 'bout to deal with him either. I mean, Kenny 'Fly' and me are about to bounce, and dog-face Colt ain't even here yet?" Nikki shrugged, then turned to check her butt in the mirror.

"Girl, I'm so fucking bored!" Tamara hollered.

"Target or not, I would not be bored up in this bitch, girl. This place is full of ballers. You besta get off your ass and leave Marleeta alone. If your nigga don't show, that's not your problem. Go work your jelly, girl. Shit, ain't no way I'd be babysitting her ass here in South Beach."

Satisfied with her appearance, Nikki gave herself another once-over in the mirror and looked at Tamara. "Well, I'll catch you all in the morning," she said. "Remember what I said, I'd catch up with her ass later."

"Hmm, I guess you're right," Tamara said as she

watched Nikki dig her shorts out of her butt before she sashayed out of the ladies' room.

Tamara stayed a little longer. She started to call Donnell but changed her mind. She decided she needed to focus on having a good time. When she went back into the club, she took her time going back to the blue bed she shared with Marleeta. She looked around at the club. Each bed was sectioned off with colored sheer curtains. She liked the atmosphere, and wished Donnell were there to see it.

After peeking in on several groups in bed, she made her way back to the blue bed, where Marleeta was still chatting away on the phone. She had a drink in one hand and was rubbing her thighs with the other.

From a distance she looked pretty funny, because she used a wireless earpiece that was discreetly attached to her ear beneath her hair. If you didn't know she was on the phone, you would've thought the woman was crazy, feeling herself up as she mumbled to no one.

Tamara planned to tell Marleeta she was about to mingle for a little while, but when she got back to the bed and picked up her glass, she was shocked.

"I gotta go," she heard Marleeta suddenly say, and jump up from the bed.

When Tamara followed Marleeta's stare to the yellow bedroom, she nearly dropped her own glass.

JD immediately regretted fucking Nikki. He knew that he let his weakness get the best of him. He also knew he was thinking with the wrong head, but he just couldn't resist Nikki's phat ass. She was a freak for real. If all went as planned, Marleeta would never find out, and his plan might still have a chance.

He only brought John to South Beach, he didn't feel like hearing Eddie's mouth. "She a cold piece, dawg, a cold piece," he'd say. So JD left Eddie back in LA to hold down the fort. When they pulled up to B.E.D., the bouncer knew JD by name.

"JD, dawg, why didn't you holla? How long you been in town?"

"Oh man, just here for a minute. Got some business to tend to," JD said as they were led into the club.

When JD walked past the pink bed and saw Nikki getting her freak on with some busta, he nudged John and they started laughing. The sight of Marleeta propped up on several pillows with a drink in her hand ended JD's laughter right away.

Their eyes connected for a quick second, and he watched as she jumped up from the bed. JD strolled past freaky Nikki and stepped up to Marleeta.

"Say, baby girl, whassup?"

Marleeta looked like she just saw a ghost. First she shook her head as if that would make him disappear. When that didn't work, she shrugged. "Ah, JD, um, hey, whassup?" she responded.

"*Daayyuum,* is that any way to greet a nigga you once had love for?" JD shook his head to the side and tsked.

Marleeta looked around nervously. She glanced at Tamara, who was still sitting on the blue bed. Nikki and Kenny "Fly" were a few feet away, tongue wrestling.

"Oh, um, hey, JD," Marleeta said as she moved in to give him a half-ass hug.

"*Daaayuum,* if a nigga didn't know any better, I'd say you wasn't happy to see me," he said.

Marleeta flipped her hair away from her ear. "Yeah, I need to go. But I'll catch up with you later."

"Oh," JD said.

Marleeta hugged JD again. This time she used her hands to travel up his back, shoulders, then down to his hips. She held her arms around his waist. "I'm sorry, boo, you caught me wrapping up an awkward conversation." She kissed his cheek and stepped back. "Whassup, John?" She smirked.

"Whadya say we get outta here," JD said.

Marleeta looked around. "Ah, naw, I can't leave with you," she said.

"Ah, why?" he asked, mocking her.

"Well, 'cause I drove. And my girls, ah, well, you know how that is." Marleeta shrugged and looked at Tamara.

Tamara got up and made her way to Marleeta's side. John reached out and smacked her on the ass.

"Excuse you," Tamara said, rolling her eyes.

"C'mon, why don't the four of us get outta here and we can show you around South Beach," John said.

"With that tired-ass line, nigga, please. You betta step off," Tamara said. She rolled her eyes and turned toward Marleeta. "So whassup, Queenie? We 'bout to bounce or what?" Tamara asked.

Before Marleeta had a chance to respond, two women came up to JD.

"Pappi," the first one screamed. "You said you'd call

next time you came to South Beach. How long you
been here?" With her head twisting, she mean mugged
Marleeta and Tamara. "Who the fuck are they?"

"Oh, don't even trip. We were just about to leave,"
Marleeta said. She quickly grabbed Tamara's arm and
they moved on. From across the club, she watched as
JD and the woman had a heated discussion.

"Let's get outta here," she said to Tamara.

Something Just Ain't Right

The next day, Marleeta nearly dropped her plate of food in the hotel's restaurant. She couldn't believe she was bumping into JD again. This time, she was able to sneak out before he saw her. Rushing back up to their room, she was baffled by these chance meetings. Once in the room, she sat there trying to figure out exactly how to deal with him.

When Tamara stepped out of the bathroom, she jumped at the sight of Marleeta. "Aeey, I thought you were eating downstairs."

"I was, but strangest thing. Guess who the fuck I bumped into, or nearly bumped into, downstairs."

"Who?" Tamara asked as she sat next to Marleeta on the couch.

"JD's ass."

"What? Again? What the fuck, that nigga following you or something?"

"Girl, it's the strangest thing. He didn't see me. I got outta there with a quickness, but how the fuck?" she said.

"Yeah, even if it was a fluke, running into him at

the club, for him to show up at our hotel? Ain't no fucking way," Tamara said. "It ain't like we up the block in LA. Shit, we in South Beach, Miami!"

"This shit is strange," Marleeta said. "You heard from Nikki yet?"

"Nah, I guess she still with Kenny 'Fly.'" Tamara snickered.

"I didn't know he was an ass man," Marleeta blurted out.

"What's been up with you lately? It's like you slipping on the job. The old Queenie would've known something like that. She would've planned for it, and she would've made sure we had two targets, not just one," Tamara said cautiously.

"I just . . . Shit, I guess I got some stuff on my mind." Marleeta shrugged. "I don't know, you guys been talking about me, huh?"

When Tamara looked at the floor, Marleeta knew her answer. Damn, had she been that off? She knew it was Zack—that dick, that tongue. How could a boy know how to please a woman like that?

"I mean, what's going on, Queenie? We ain't never seen you like this before. It's like you done switched up on us. We all notice the difference," Tamara said.

"I guess I'm just looking at the end. I mean, I don't want to do this shit forever. I got plans for the future. I'm just stacking my cash," she offered.

"Yeah, but, Queenie, if we gonna do it, we need to do it right. Otherwise, shit, anything could happen. I know I don't have to tell you what we do for a living, right?" Tamara said.

"I don't know what's come over me. I'll tell you

this. In about six or seven months, I don't wanna be doing this shit. That for real," Marleeta confessed.

When Tamara started shaking her head, Marleeta didn't know what to think. "What?"

Tamara smiled. "Are you serious?" she asked.

"Yeah. I didn't want to say anything, 'cause I didn't want you guys slacking off. You know Headhunters is real close to my heart, but I ain't trying to make this a career." Marleeta looked at her. "If you want, girl, you could take over, but I know I've been saving my money, and I'm . . . well . . . Let's just say I got plans."

"*Daaayuuum,* girl, Queenie, I feel so much better!" Tamara exclaimed.

"What? Whassup?" Marleeta asked, confusion all across her face.

"I didn't know how to tell you, but I'm out in six months too. On the real. I was trying to figure out how to break the news to you, because I didn't want to leave you stuck. Girl, I hope Nikki and the boys been saving up, 'cause I'm with you. This shit is cool and all, but from day one I knew this wouldn't last forever. When Trey got shot, I knew the end was close for me."

"I need to keep my head on straight for the time being, though. Refocus and shit," Marleeta resolved.

"Yeah, you do," Tamara added. "Look, I don't know what's up with you and this nigga JD, but I'm ready to eat, and I ain't trying to stay locked up in this room. Why you scared of that nigga anyway? You think he found out we got him?"

"Nah, it's not that." Marleeta looked at the floor.

"What is it then?" Tamara pressed.

"Well, that nigga was starting to get attached. You

know, it was just a job for me, but it was like we started playing house, and he got comfortable, I got comfortable. Then my ass went back to work. So, I don't know, it's like I didn't want to string him along, so I just cut things off, cold turkey."

"*Wwhhhhat?* You mean to tell me that nigga is sprung off the cat? Shit, girl, please quit hiding from that nigga. Let him get a whiff, then make him pay. Now I know something is wrong with you, 'cause the old Queenie would've milked that nigga for every red cent she could get her hands on. What, you done found a conscience?" Tamara giggled.

"Girl, nah, but I ain't trying to string this nigga along either. He ain't nothing nice. And, shit, I wanna make it out of this—not only alive, but, shit, I'm trying to retire in Belize. A bitch still want to look good. You know, try to get me a lil' young Rasta man," Marleeta joked.

"Okay, here's what I'm saying. Queenie, that nigga is following you. He's gotta be. So I say, take his fucking money, he's all but begging you to. I feel you, about what you were saying, but he's begging for it. So I say, do what you gotta do. Now, c'mon, let's go eat!"

When Tamara and Marleeta walked out of their room and rounded the corner, Marleeta nearly passed out at the sight of JD. He was leaning up against a door, as if he were listening for voices.

"Oh snap," he said.

Marleeta and Tamara looked at each other, then at him.

"Ah, I lost my room key, and I, ah, forgot what

room I'm in, so I was listening for my boy John." He eased into step with them.

Marleeta shrugged. "You ain't gotta explain nothing to me," she said.

"Hmm, I don't want y'all to think I'm some kind of freak. And, shit, you know peeping in people's rooms to get off, or some sick shit like that."

"Uh-huh," Tamara mumbled. Marleeta shrugged.

"Well, it's a damn shame you not a freak," Tamara said. She nudged Marleeta. "'Cause my girl here got a serious weakness for freaks." She giggled.

Marleeta laughed. JD laughed too. He stared at her longingly as they stood waiting for the elevator.

Marleeta wanted to ask where the hell he was going, but she figured he'd soon get off the elevator at his floor and move on. When the elevator stopped on the fourth floor and a white couple stepped on and JD didn't move, she hid her disappointment.

"Mornin'," the man said. He nodded toward the three of them.

"Hello," Marleeta mumbled. Tamara and JD kept their eyes on the numbers that lined the top of the elevator cab.

When the door opened in the lobby, Tamara and Marleeta stepped off and stood for a second before walking toward the restaurant.

The moment they stopped, JD stopped.

"I'm 'bout to go get some grub. I don't know 'bout y'all, but a nigga's starving," he said. He rubbed his stomach for good measure.

"Hmm," was all Marleeta could manage. She hoped her face didn't betray her and reveal the complete shock she felt at that moment.

Just as they were about to leave, with JD trailing closely behind, the elevator doors opened again. John rushed out.

"I couldn't find her. . . ." His voice trailed off when JD turned and he saw Marleeta and Tamara. Now Marleeta knew for sure, he had been following her, stalking almost. She had to find out why, and just exactly what the fuck he wanted.

JD had seen Marleeta duck out of the restaurant. He was determined to catch up with her, but he couldn't move fast enough. He had tried to pay off the desk clerks, but still they wouldn't reveal her room number. He wasn't even sure what he would do once he found her. Things were changing. At first, he promised to deal with her ever so severely, but the more he chased, the more he became intrigued by her and her brilliance. He couldn't get thoughts of her off his mind.

Even as his little Cuban honey was sucking his dick the night before, he kept imagining it was Marleeta. By the time she had swallowed, he was uninterested in what she had to offer. His mind was glued to Marleeta. He wanted to know if she was working or just in South Beach to play.

A part of him wanted to be a mark again, just so he could be in her company. But he knew that wasn't possible. After he got rid of Lucy, he made it his business to try and find Marleeta. He would've gotten the information from Nikki, but the bitch wasn't answering her cell phone. He'd deal with her ass later, he thought.

Then, as luck would have it, he decided to get breakfast, and there she was. She thought he didn't see her, but how could he not? When his every waking thought was about her, he could almost sense when she was near.

When she slipped out of the restaurant, he was right behind her, but he lost her.

JD immediately dialed John's number and told him to meet in the lobby. Once there, he explained to John that they needed to search every floor until they found which room Marleeta was staying in.

John looked at JD. "You serious, dawg?"

"Hell yeah, what you think?"

"So you want me to go and search each floor of this hotel looking for this bitch? Whassup, man? It don't seem to me like this is about revenge anymore."

"Look, nigga, it ain't like we in a twenty-story building. I'll start at the top. I'll take floors six through four. You start down here and work your way up. I'll meet you back here in about, what, two hours?"

Before John could muster another word, JD hopped on the elevator and rode it up to the sixth floor. Oh, he'd find her, no matter what. When he got off on the sixth floor, a group of white old ladies wearing matching red shirts walked past him. They entered the rooms to the left of the elevator, so that saved him a trip. He knew those were occupied.

JD turned to the right. There were three rooms in that row, with two suites around the corner. He pressed his ear up against the first door and heard nothing. At the next door, he heard screams of passion, but it wasn't Marleeta's voice. At the last door, he thought he heard the TV, but he couldn't tell for sure.

He pressed his body up against the door, as if that would help him hear better. He closed his eyes, hoping to force his ears to work better. When he opened his eyes and saw Marleeta and Tamara walking by, he tried to jump back, but it was too late.

JD wanted to tell her that he had been searching for her. He wanted to tell her they needed to go somewhere and talk, but the look on her face said this wasn't the time. What about dealing with her ever so severely? A small voice in his head nagged. *"She a cold piece,"* he heard Eddie's voice howl. His plans were to make her suffer. But he had to be honest with himself. The only suffering he wanted to see her doing was the kind that had her screaming for more.

JD shook the thoughts off, and said the first thing that popped into his head. He knew they wouldn't buy his lame-ass excuse about losing his room key, but what the fuck? He had found Marleeta and he'd be damned if he let her get away again.

Now he just had to figure out what the hell to do with her.

Nikki rolled over in Kenny's California king-sized four-poster bed. She had been lying on his nine-hundred-thread-count Egyptian cotton sheets for the last three days, and she didn't care if she ever saw Marleeta, Tamara, or the boys again.

She had found her soul mate, a man who had a fond appreciation for the booty, and he didn't mind letting her know—her ass was all that, and then some. He had treated her like the real queen the moment she stepped into his waterfront house. Kenny lived lavish, and Nikki loved that about him.

From fine art to fine furniture, and his all-white

bedroom, she had never felt so good about herself or any man. She knew she should've called to check in, but, shit, she didn't feel like it. Nikki had turned her phone off long ago, and she didn't care if she ever turned it on again. She would marry Kenny if he asked—hell, she might even ask him.

Stretched out on her back, with her legs wide open, she was watching music videos on his thirty-six-inch plasma screen TV, which was mounted on the wall at the foot of the bed. The sheets felt like a smooth and creamy lotion next to her skin. "Yeah, I could get used to this," she said.

"I'm glad to hear that, boo." When she looked up, Kenny was carrying a tray with food stacked high. "I thought you might not want to get out of bed again today, so I'm bringing the food to you. Let's eat, then do what we do best." He smiled.

Nikki liked everything about him. He knew how to touch her, make her feel like a woman, keep her screaming through the night, then have her purring until the wee hours of the morning. Yes, she had finally found her Mister Right. She didn't give a damn about anything or anyone else. And she knew he felt the same way too.

Kenny told Nikki he had a woman before she came along, but when he saw her, he knew he had to have her. When she accused him of bumping his gums and trying to make her feel good, he picked up the phone and started dialing. After a few minutes, he pushed a button and a female's voice filled the room.

"Say, Mercedes, whassup?"

"Nothing, Kenny. Where you been? You ain't answering your cellie. If I didn't know any better, I woulda thought the feds picked you up. Why you ain't called me?"

"It's worse than the feds, baby girl," he said.

"What? What could be worse than that?"

"I met your replacement two days ago," he said.

"Um, what? What did you just say?" Mercedes asked, her voice laced with much attitude.

"I said, I met your replacement two days ago. That's why you ain't heard from me. A nigga in love," Kenny said, winking at Nikki.

"Nigga, I know you best stop playing with my emotions. *That shit ain't even funny,*" Mercedes hissed.

"Nikki, am I bullshittin' or what?"

"Nah, Daddy, you on point, for real," Nikki said toward the speakerphone.

"*Whaaat?* Who the fuck is that bitch? Oh no she didn't, Kenneth. I'm on my way over there right now. I want you to tell me this shit to my face!"

"It was the ass, Mercedes. Nikki got a ass, like *Bam*! It was that ass that did me in. Baby, you knew what you was getting yourself into from jump. Don't hate, just congratulate, 'cause I don' found my real boo." Kenny and Nikki fell out laughing.

"Nigga, no you didn't! Uh-uh, we gon' see about this shit. I'm on my way!" she warned again.

"Kenny, what if she come over here acting the fool and shit?"

"Ah, girl, don't even trip. Mercedes ain't crazy, she'll be a'ight! Now give me some of that ass I left my girl for," he said.

"Come and get it, baby! It's all yours!" Nikki cooed.

* * *

Every time Nikki thought about that shit, she couldn't help but crack up. Kenny changed the channel to a hot flick and they lay back on the bed. As they eased back to feed each other, Nikki thought she smelled something.

Convinced it was just her mind fucking with her, she pushed the tray to the side and looked at her man. "I'm still hungry, but I don't want any more food," she said with a devilish grin.

"Say no more, boo," Kenny said.

Although it was midafternoon, he pushed a button that closed a pair of massive drapes. When darkness enveloped the room, Nikki ignored her senses and grabbed Kenny's bald head as he went between her thighs.

"Damn, it's getting hot in here. You didn't leave the stove on, did you?"

"Oh, it's getting hot, all right," he said as he briefly looked up from between her legs.

One final suck sent her over the top. Nikki and Kenny were in the zone. But the loud buzzing noise jolted them both up and out of the bed. Nikki looked up and screamed, *"Ohmigod!* Where is all that smoke coming from?"

Kenny jumped up to see smoke quickly seeping beneath his bedroom door. "Oh shit! Is the house on fire?" He quickly grabbed a pair of shorts. "C'mon, boo, I think we gotta get outta here. Damn, the house is on fire!"

Nikki scrambled for a T-shirt, since she couldn't find her clothes. In the distance, she could hear sirens blaring, but the room started getting hotter. Within seconds, they were coughing as Kenny tried to kick out the window.

The phone started ringing. When kicking didn't work, he pulled one of his nightstands away from the wall.

"Hurry, Kenny," Nikki begged.

As he scrambled to remove the drawers so he could lift it, a voice filled the room.

"Hmm, bet things are heating up for you and my replacement, huh?"

That was the last thing they heard before Kenny took Nikki's hand and they jumped out of the second-story window.

Confessions

After they ate, Marleeta, Tamara, and JD walked out of the restaurant and into the lobby. Marleeta was tired of Tamara's glances that seemed to say, *Ah, can't you do something to get rid of him?* The last time she got that look, she shrugged.

"So you been to South Beach before?" Marleeta heard JD ask.

As he spoke, she kept trying to think of ways to get rid of him. They had endured his lame-ass conversation through a late lunch. And, truthfully, she was wondering where the hell Nikki's ass was.

When she saw that JD wasn't trying to leave, they moved toward the big-screen TV in the lobby.

"Oh shit! Girl, that's Nikki," Tamara said, pointing at the TV screen.

Marleeta turned away from JD. "Shit, what's going on? What are they talking about?" She glanced around the room. "Where's the remote? Can we get some volume on this?"

JD walked over and flipped a panel beneath the screen. He hit a button and raised the volume on the

TV. It was the news. A reporter stood in front of a burning house.

"What the hell?" Tamara screamed.

"Sssssssh!" Marleeta stared at the screen.

"Police have detained a young woman, Mercedes Alvarez, in connection with the arson. They say a domestic dispute may have led to all of this. At the time the fire broke out, Alvarez's boyfriend and another woman had to jump out of a window to safety."

The camera showed an image of Kenny "Fly," with his arm around Nikki, at the back of an ambulance.

"Snap! And here I was wondering where the fuck Nikki was. A fire?"

Marleeta looked at Tamara and sighed. "I wonder what part of town they're in. It don't look like she's going to the hospital," she said.

"Oh, I know exactly where that is. Here, I can take you if you want," he offered.

Marleeta looked at him.

"What? You don't trust me now all of a sudden?" he asked. "Just c'mon up to my room with me so I can get my keys and shit and we can bounce," JD said.

Tamara looked at Marleeta. "You go on, I'll stay here in case she calls," she said.

"Okay, well, make sure you call my cell if you hear from her," Marleeta said.

As she rode the elevator up to the fifth floor, she started wondering what this meant for business. No way in hell were they gonna be able to pull anything off if the nigga's house burned down. They walked into JD's room. Marleeta looked around as he walked to the back. "You want a drink?"

Did she hear him correctly? A drink? Wasn't they supposed to be headed to pick Nikki up? A drink? And what the hell was taking him so damn long anyway?

"Nah, I'm straight." She turned the TV on, but she couldn't remember which channel was broadcasting the fire.

A few minutes later, JD walked back into the living room. "Shit, a nigga can't even find his keys." He patted his pockets.

Marleeta looked up at him. She looked around the room again. "What you mean you can't find your keys?" She glanced toward the door. JD moved back a few steps. Marleeta looked at him. She got up from her spot on the sofa. "Well, I better get outta here. Shit, I got a car. I just thought since you knew where you were going . . . hell, we can take my car." She started toward the door.

Before she reached for the handle, JD grabbed her arm. "Wait, I need to tell you something," he said.

Marleeta didn't move. She wasn't ready for this shit, she needed to go and see about Nikki. That was her money; that was *the* reason they were in South Beach. She'd hear him out, tell him whatever the hell he wanted to hear, and get outta there as fast as possible.

"What is it, JD?" she asked without turning around to face him.

"Fuck Nikki," he said.

Marleeta remained silent. Damn, she wasn't in the mood for this shit. She sighed. The grip on her arm tightened a bit, but she told herself not to panic. She closed her eyes. "What's that supposed to mean?" she asked.

JD walked around to see her face. He stood between

her and the door. He reached for her face and took it between the palms of his hands. "Don't worry about Nikki. She can handle herself," he said.

Marleeta was more confused than afraid. She didn't understand what was going on, but she'd play it cool. She'd hear him out; then she'd leave. That's what she'd do. "Hmm," Marleeta mumbled.

JD took her by the arm and led her to the bedroom. Marleeta didn't want to panic. She could handle JD, she wasn't about to start worrying about his ass. She nearly gasped when she looked around the bedroom. There were candles everywhere! She didn't know what to say or do. "Is this what you were doing back here?"

He nodded his head and rubbed his hands against her shoulders. "I've been waiting for this moment since you up and walked away from a nigga. I'm mad in love with you, girl."

"You're what?" Marleeta managed. *Love?* Where the hell did that come from? And what should she say? All she could think about was Zack. Where was he? What was he doing? He and the boys were supposed to roll into town in a few days. It was supposed to be Trey's first day back. She could work this. And if she had to fuck him to get outta there, then Zack and everybody else would just have to understand.

"C'mon, girl, you know we were on to something real tight." He shrugged. "I don't know what a nigga did to set you off, but we coulda worked it out, huh?"

"Oh nah, it ain't even like that. I mean, it wasn't is all I'm saying." She looked around the room again. He was too close. She didn't know how to back away from him, and Lord knows she didn't want to piss him off.

Marleeta eased beyond his grip and walked over to the bed. She sat down and leaned back a bit. "So you wanted me here, I'm here—what's up? What's going on? What you want? Some ass?" she asked.

"It's more than that. I mean, you stay on a nigga's mind, and shit. I want you, girl. I really do," he said.

Marleeta spread her legs just so. "Well, you got me, Daddy, I'm right here. Whassup?"

JD shook his head. "Don't play me, Queen. That's not what I'm talking about. You ain't gotta play a brotha."

"I don't know what you want from me. You got me up in here in this romantic-ass setting, and, shit, now you acting like you don't want to get down. Do you even know what you want, JD? Just tell me what you want," she cooed.

"Damn, girl." He stroked his crotch. "Damn, you got a nigga all twisted in the head. You know I want you, for real, but not just like that. I mean . . ." He sighed and shook his head.

Marleeta took his hand. She moved it to her face and placed two of his fingers into her mouth. She sucked and sucked his fingers until he released a deep growl.

"*Sssssssss,* see, Daddy, lemme make you feel better," she whispered. Marleeta got up and rubbed her hands on his shoulders. She took a deep breath. "I'ma make it all better for you, but you gotta trust me, 'kay?" she said.

JD hadn't uttered another word. He threw his head back and relished the moment. Her hands felt so good on his body. Then, when she pulled his shirt up, showing his rippled chest, he didn't know what to do.

Marleeta kissed him softly. She licked his stomach, then started gyrating on his leg.

"*Oooh, girl!* Wait!" he begged, actually backing away from her.

Marleeta's nostrils flared. She exhaled and looked around the room. She shook her head. "Damn, JD, whassup?" she asked.

"Queen, I want you and shit, but I need to make sure ain't no niggas gonna bust up in here, with pistols blazing," he said.

Marleeta looked at him. "What the hell is that supposed to mean?"

He walked up to her and looked in her eyes. "Look, I need to know if you gonna be down with a nigga for real."

"JD, either you wanna fuck or you gonna let me outta here. It's that simple, I got things to do," she said.

"Oh yeah? Hmmm." JD smiled. "You got business, huh?"

Smack!

Marleeta's head snapped back from the slap. Her face was stinging, but she refused to let him see her shed a single tear.

"You think I don't know? Bitch, if you wanted money, all you had to do was ask. You ain't have to play with a nigga's feelings, then rob me! What? You thought I wasn't gonna find out?" he screamed.

Marleeta looked horrified.

"So when am I coming to sunny LA?" Donnell's voice asked.

Tamara rolled her eyes. She could be lying up with

her man instead of sitting up in a hotel room in South Beach waiting for Nikki's ass to call. She hoped Marleeta would slap the shit out of Nikki once she and JD found her ass.

That bitch Nikki had the audacity to have them sitting up worrying about her ass, while she was kicking it in a waterfront mansion. *Shit, they should've burned in that bitch,* Tamara thought.

"Babe, I'm not in LA right now. I'm out of town on business," Tamara said.

"Oh, why didn't you tell me? I thought you were at home, just running the streets," he joked.

"Nah, boo, I'm not even in Cali."

"Well, when you getting back?" he asked.

"Hmm, that's a good question. I thought we'd be here for two weeks, but looks like we may be here longer. I don't know yet," she confessed.

"Damn, a whole 'nother week or longer? Shit, I might as well come there then. I needs to see you, girl!"

"I know, right?"

"Well, shit, let's make it happen, then."

Tamara sat up. She looked around the empty hotel room. She didn't need this shit. Truth be told, she had enough money to last her long enough to flip it and live comfortably anyway. Why shouldn't her man come be by her side? Her target never even showed up.

"You know what? That might not be a bad idea at all," she said into the phone.

"Say, why don't I call the airlines. If the ticket's not too much, then I could meet you down there on my next day off," Donnell offered.

"So when you off again?" she asked.

"Day after tomorrow, Thursday, gotta be back Sunday," he said.

"Shit, that would be cool," Tamara said. "I'll get us a room," she offered.

"Hell, why can't I just stay where you are now?" he asked.

"Oh, I'm here with my business partners. Don't trip, I'll take care of the ticket and the room."

"Nah, baby, I ain't 'bout to let you pick up the tab," he insisted. "What kind of chump you take me for?" he asked.

"Don't even trip. I can write it off as a business expense," she lied.

Two hours later, Donnell called back with his flight information. He told Tamara he'd be at the Miami International Airport, Thursday night, at nine forty-five.

She knew she probably should've given it more thought before inviting him down or allowing him to invite himself. But, shit, why shouldn't she have some fun? So far, all she'd been doing was sitting around Miami watching everyone else have a ball. Shit, she wasn't even working. Tamara decided she'd tell Marleeta right away. No use in letting it pop up on them. She searched through her phone's call log and pushed a button to dial Marleeta.

The phone rang about seven times before voice mail finally kicked in. Frustrated, Tamara dialed her number again. When the voice mail clicked on yet again, she flipped on the television to see if the news crew had any more coverage about the fire. They had seen it on the noon broadcast, quite surely somebody was about to have some news, she thought as she flipped through the channels.

When she couldn't find news on any of the stations in the room, she figured she'd call Nikki's cell phone. When she didn't get an answer there either, she decided to walk down to the lobby.

"I'm in a room upstairs, but I need another room for Thursday night through Saturday night." She waited as the clerk typed on the computer.

"Mmm, I have something, but it's just a regular single," the woman said as she typed.

"That'll work," Tamara said.

"You want me to bill it to your current room?" the clerk asked.

"No, I'll pay for that in cash." She reached for her purse.

"Oh no, ma'am, you pay when you check out."

"Okay," Tamara said.

"You can check in anytime after three," the clerk said.

Tamara had no idea where Marleeta had gone off to, and she sure as hell didn't know what was up with Nikki. Shit, she wished Donnell could've come sooner. As she was about to step out of the hotel lobby, her cell phone rang.

"It's about damn time," she said, hitting the talk button. "What the fuck is going on?" Tamara screamed.

"That's what I'm trying to find out," the man's voice answered back.

"Zack? That you?"

"Yeah, who was you expecting? Where the hell is Queenie?" he asked.

"*Umph,* ain't no telling. She left with JD, what, five hours ago now, and I ain't heard from her ass yet. She was supposed to go see about Nikki's ass. She and her target had to jump out a window when his house caught fire."

"Wait, slow up, slow up," Zack said.

Tamara paused. "Okay, well, that's what's up. I thought you was either Nikki or Queenie's ass. I'm tired of hanging out in South Beach by my goddamn self!"

"You said Queenie went with JD, where they go? And what the fuck is JD doing there in South Beach?" Zack asked.

"I don't know, but what I do know is one of 'em needs to call me, 'cause I'm tired of sitting around this hotel by myself," she whined.

"Why did you let her go with him? I don't understand what he's doing there. How long he been there?" he hammered.

"Who are you talking about?"

"JD! Didn't you say Queenie went off with him? Where are they? I don't understand," he said.

"Zack, you on one, huh? What do you care if Queenie is off with JD? Knowing her, she probably hitting that nigga up as we speak. You know she ain't giving it up for free," Tamara joked.

"That shit ain't funny, Tamara. He could be doing something to her ass and you got jokes. Shit, you need to go find her."

"Zack, why you sweating Queenie so hard? Whassup with—" Tamara stopped midsentence. "Wait one fucking minute here!" she screamed. "You fucking Queenie?" She stormed over to the bank of elevators.

"Zack, I know you heard me, you and Queenie fucking or what?" Tamara smashed the up button for the elevator. "I know you heard me, boy!" she screamed.

Nikki always dreamt of being on TV, but never like this. Yeah, she enjoyed *Jerry Springer,* but she wasn't trying to be caught up in no shit that would be ideal for his talk show. Yet, here she was, caught on camera running from a burning house after her new man's deranged hoochie set the place ablaze.

"Don't even worry about this shit, baby girl. I'ma take you shopping to replace your old shit. Then we gonna head outta here. You wanna go to Destin? I got a place on the beach there," he offered.

"Kenny, I really need to catch up to my girls, or at least check in with them. I know they worried 'bout my ass," Nikki said.

The truth was, she wanted to make sure he was really through with Mercedes's ass. That bitch was seriously unstable. She hadn't known Kenny for a good week and she was going through this kind of shit with him.

"Why don't I take you back to your girls—I'll take y'all out to eat. Then, if they give you the thumbs-up on me, we can bounce. But first, let's go get you some new clothes and shit." Kenny tugged on the T-shirt she was still wearing.

A woman from the Red Cross had come to offer assistance, until she noticed the sprawling property. "What she want?" Nikki had asked Kenny as the woman approached.

"She was probably gonna give you a Wal-Mart

voucher for some clothes and shit. You don't need no handouts, babe," he had assured her.

When she and Kenny "Fly" pulled up at the hotel, Nikki convinced him to let her go up to the room. She told him to give her a few minutes with her girls; then she'd call him up when they were ready.

"Well, at least lemme get you some help up with all these bags," he said.

"Okay, I'll be right back. Why don't you go wait in the bar, have a drink, and I'll put on one of my new outfits and meet you back here in twenty minutes."

Kenny held her hand in his. "Twenty?" he asked.

"Sooner, if you let me hurry and go," she promised.

A bellboy helped Nikki up to the room. When she opened the door and found Tamara pacing the floor, she quickly tipped him and closed the door. She wheeled the cart in, carrying all of the things they'd purchased.

"What's wrong with you?" she asked Tamara.

"Oh, you finally remembered you weren't here alone, huh?"

"Girl, don't trip. I need to talk to Queenie's ass." Nikki looked around the room, toward the back. "She here?"

"Nah, I ain't seen her ass since they went looking for you. Shit, that was earlier this morning. Now it's, what, damn near ten o'clock at night? I ain't heard from her or you!"

"Shit, girl, calm down. What you all twisted up about?" Nikki asked.

"How about, I think Zack is fucking Queenie?"

Tamara tossed out. "I've been trying to find her ass for the past three hours, ever since I talked to Zack, but she ain't answering her phone."

"*Whhhaaat?* She fucking your lil' cousin?" Nikki asked.

"Well, he ain't that little, but, still, I don't want Queenie to get his head all fucked up and shit. Of all the niggas we come across, why she have to fuck with him? And what happened to all that shit about not mixing business and pleasure?"

"See, that's what I've been trying to tell you about her. The rules are etched in stone when it comes to our asses, yet she feel like she could do whatever the fuck she want, and nothing!" Nikki added. She shook her head. "That's fucked up. What Zack say when you confronted him about it?"

"Well, he didn't deny it. He didn't admit it either. He just hung up on me. You know they on their way here now."

Nikki nodded. "Hmm, where is she anyway?" she asked.

"I told you, she left with that nigga JD to find you after we saw you on the news. I ain't seen her ass since!" Tamara picked up her phone and again dialed Marleeta's number. This time, her voice mail was full. She had already left a good ten messages.

"Wait, Tamara, you didn't say she was with JD. How long you say they been gone?" Nikki clarified.

"Um, I said they been gone for hours. Since earlier today."

Nikki was hot. No, JD didn't just use her to get to Marleeta. Their agreement was he wouldn't make a move, do a damn thing, unless she was there to witness whatever he was gonna do. Deep down, she wasn't even sure if he'd be able to pull it off; now here he was with her alone. Well, not if she had anything to say about it.

Nikki changed into one of the new sweat suits Kenny just bought and headed toward the door.

"Wait, where you going?" Tamara screamed, grabbing her key card and following behind Nikki.

"Girl, I'm going to confront Queenie and that nigga JD!"

"How? You know where they at?"

"Girl, who you think told JD's ass where to find her—hell, us. He probably got her up in his room on the fifth floor. Oh, this nigga must be crazy if he think he go' play me. I ain't even having it!" Nikki screamed.

A Hot Mess

Marleeta sat speechless. She didn't know what to do. Was he going to hurt her? Maybe he'd try to rape her? Nah, when she offered him the pussy, he didn't want it. Well, she just wanted him to do whatever he was gonna do and get it over with.

"Yeah, I know," he said. "I gotta admit, though, I had no fucking idea at first. You had me—had me feeling all bad and shit about what happened—and all along it was you and your crew. The Headhunters, isn't that right?"

Marleeta looked up at him, but she still didn't say anything.

"Y'all some bad bitches. I gotta give it to you, the way you peep a nigga out, see what he moving, pick your targets, then have your stickup boys roll in. All sweet, babe, a real nice setup you got going there. But you made a mistake when you picked a nigga like me. It wasn't even about the money. See, as my girl, you could've gotten ten times more." JD took her face into his hand as he squeezed hard. "You know, at first, I was about to deal with your ass, most severely," he said. "But the more I thought about it, and how you do what you do, well, that shit started turning me on. Then I had to find a way to get to you." His mouth swallowed hers. His tongue explored the roof of her mouth, swept over her tongue and underneath. Then he sucked the side of her neck.

"Yeah, I started dreaming about you, wondering who you was fucking, which nigga you'd be laying up with, and what you was letting them fools do to you, all for some cash." He rubbed his hands along her neck and shoulder. "It got so bad, my boys started talking about me for always talking about you. They made me promise I'd make you pay. Told me to put it on everything I love." His hand slid down the front of her tank top. He fondled her nipples, squeezing one between his index finger and his thumb.

"Yeah, I just wanted to be alone with your ass. I wanted to fuck you every way possible—shit, in your ass, your ear, your nose, your mouth, your eye, anywhere and everywhere possible," he said.

Marleeta swallowed hard. *This fool is obsessed,* she thought.

"How did you . . . ," she trailed off.

"What, find you? Find out?" He shrugged.

Marleeta nodded.

"You see, with all the research you do, all the digging, covering your bases and finding out what you can all over the country, you don't even know what's going on with the members of your crew." JD took his finger, put it in his mouth, then shoved it back down into her bra. "Yeah, your girl Nikki, that bitch got a serious gambling problem. Once I found that out, well, finding you and what you do—shit, that was easy," he said.

"Nikki," Marleeta mumbled.

"Yeah, your girl sold you out. But it cost me a pretty penny too. That bitch needs some help. I mean, she a serious gambler," JD taunted.

Marleeta hung her head. She wasn't sure what was more painful. Yet another sign that she had been slipping, or the fact that since JD was revealing all of this information, she had no idea what that meant for her.

"What do you want from me? What do you want me to do? You want your money back?"

JD snatched her by the neck. "I told you that money didn't mean shit! You didn't have to rob me, I would've given it to you. All I wanted was you, till I learned the truth."

"You can still have me," Marleeta offered. She snatched her top off. "Is that what this is all about?"

"You just don't get it. I don't want your funky ass now. You ain't nothing but a ho, and everybody know you can't turn a ho into a housewife, no matter how hard you try," JD said.

But Marleeta knew he didn't mean it. For once, she could finally see the hurt in another man's eyes. She hadn't tried since she lost Stoney. None of it was supposed to be like this.

JD released her, and Marleeta closed her eyes. JD stuck his hand under the mattress. Marleeta didn't even jump when she felt the cold metal barrel against her skin. He moved it from her cleavage, up her shoulder, and to her neck. When the barrel moved to her chin, she froze.

"You made a fool outta me," he whispered.

Marleeta felt warm tears trailing down her cheeks.

"I didn't mean to," she tried. The barrel was at her lips. JD traced the lining of her lips with the tip of his barrel.

"You didn't have to do a nigga like that. They say you a cold piece, but I wanted to believe different. And what I find you doing here in South Beach— somebody's gotta stop you, baby girl. You won't stop yourself," he said softly.

Marleeta sniffled. She didn't know what to say to that. Should she promise that if he let her go, she'd never stick up another man? Or should she just hear him out, let him talk? The gun made her nervous. Why did he want to hurt her like that?

"JD, can't we start over?" she pleaded.

"What would be the point?" he asked. "If I let you walk outta here, all you gon' do is find another nigga to stick up. You ain't gonna stop, it's all about the money for you. I know your kind," he said.

"But you love me, don't you?" Marleeta searched his eyes for any sign of how he was feeling. "You said so yourself, that you love me. What happened to that love, JD?"

He dropped the gun, startling both himself and Marleeta. She didn't know whether she should go for it, or try to run out of the room. She looked into his eyes and saw a deranged man staring back at her.

"I do love you, you just don't know," he said.

Marleeta reached down for the gun, but JD snapped out of it and jumped on top of her. They wrestled, tumbling back and forth, until the gun went off.

* * *

Tamara was hot on Nikki's tail as she stormed out of the room. "Uh-uh, where are you going?" she asked, struggling to keep up with Nikki. When Tamara thought of finding Marleeta, she wondered how she'd confront her boss about fucking her cousin.

Yeah, Zack was damn near grown, but Tamara knew how Marleeta went through men. She was all about the cash, and wasn't trying to change. Tamara didn't want her cousin to get hurt. Hadn't they just talked about the future? Hadn't Marleeta confessed she was trying to stack her paper so she could bounce and leave the States behind? What would happen to her cousin once she did that?

When Tamara finally caught up to Nikki at the bank of elevators, she stepped in front of her and slammed her into the wall. "Now, look, you are gonna tell me what the fuck is going on!" she screamed.

"Wait, just wait. I'll explain everything later. I just need to find Queenie and JD."

"What did you mean back there, when you said you two had an agreement? What fucking agreement? What is going on, Nikki? I swear to God, if you don't tell me something now, I'ma slam your head through this fucking wall!"

"It's a long story," Nikki cried, struggling to free herself from Tamara.

"Then make it short!"

By the time the elevator rang and opened its doors, Zack, Trey, and Danny Boy stumbled off and into the hall.

"What the fuck is going on? Where's Queenie?" Zack asked. He looked at Nikki, then at Tamara.

"We 'bout to go get that bitch right now!" Nikki yelled.

Zack jumped in her face. "I ain't gonna let you disrespect my woman like that, Nikki," he warned. Danny Boy, Trey, and Tamara all stared at him.

"Your woman? Since when?" Trey asked. "Damn, a nigga go down for a minute and, shit, just goes buck wild around this bitch."

Tamara was fuming. She shoved her cousin. "Why would you fuck with Queenie? You know how cold she is. Boy, what's wrong with you?"

"She ain't even like that," Zack defended.

Tamara looked at Nikki. "If you know where the fuck they are, you better get to talking right now." She snapped her finger. "I'm this close to whupping your ass, Nikki. I went to bat for your ass with Queenie. Bitch, you was broke and on your last leg when we rescued you."

"Rescued? Yo, you better step off, you talking mad shit right now. I know you hot and shit, but it's your girl Queenie you mad at, not me. I'm not the one fucking your lil' cousin."

"I'm a grown-ass man, I can fuck whoever I want. You need to tell us where to find Queenie. And I swear, if that nigga touched a hair on her body, I'll kill you with my bare hands!"

Nikki looked at him. "You think she wants you? Please, you just a lil' boy toy to her. Think about it, she fucks for money. But whatever!" She flicked her hand and pressed the down button.

When a car opened, they piled into the elevator and got off on the fifth floor. Nikki looked to the left, then to the right. "Shit, I don't remember what room he's in."

"You forgot which room he's in?" Tamara screamed. "You got some serious explaining to do when this shit is all said and done," Tamara warned.

"Explaining?" Zack said. "I know Queenie better be all right."

"Shit, lemme think," Nikki said, looking down the hall in both directions.

A few minutes later, a gunshot rang out from a room a few feet down. They turned to the right and ran down the hall.

"Oh shit!" Zack yelled.

"It came from the room in the middle," Danny Boy said.

They started banging on the door. "Queenie! Queenie! Are you in there?"

Nikki stood back, her hands covering her face.

The End of the Road

By the time security made it up to room 508, the door was hanging on two of its three hinges. The police were right behind them. Tamara was upset beyond words after seeing the look on her cousin's face when he found a half-naked Marleeta on the floor with JD. Danny Boy and Trey weren't comfortable around the police, so they were glad when they were asked to wait out in the hall.

Nikki stood in the hall between the bathroom and bedroom and was interviewed by a police officer.

Officers took pictures of the finger marks around Marleeta's neck, the bruise on the side of her face, and her torn clothes. JD's body lay lifeless, a few feet away.

A detective was questioning Marleeta about what had happened, for the third time. Her story never changed. She told them she had to shoot JD to save herself. She said they struggled for the gun after he had tried to rape her. No, the gun was not hers. No, she had no idea he was a felon in possession of a firearm. They put brown paper bags on her hands and informed her that she'd have to go downtown for more questioning.

It didn't take long for Kenny to follow all of the commotion up to the fifth floor. When he tried to get to Nikki, officers asked him to wait in the hall. As he stood back, he wondered if she was worth the headache he was sure surrounded the mess he was looking at. When everyone seemed busy and wrapped up in the situation, he eased down the hall and back to the elevator. As he waited, he decided he'd lose her number.

Six months later . . .

Marleeta sat back on her lounge chair. The swooshing sound of the waves as they splashed ashore was relaxing and therapeutic. She chuckled as she read the words on the piece of paper she held. Tamara kept the letters coming. She said it was her way of making Marleeta feel like she wasn't far from home.

Marleeta had learned that Tamara had moved to Houston and was running a string of salons with her fiancé. They were planning a spring wedding at Marleeta's house in Belize next year. Danny Boy and Trey had moved to Atlanta. It seemed they pooled their money from the Headhunters and were going into the music-producing business. One of their groups was already signed up to entertain at Tamara's wedding. Marleeta couldn't wait to host the wedding party for Tamara. She looked around her property and smiled at everything she owned. From her deck in the backyard, Marleeta was less than twenty feet from the beautiful Belizean beachfront.

"I can't believe that skank Nikki is really out tricking. It don't make no sense that she didn't save one dime of that money," she said.

"Yeah, well, that's how it happens sometimes."

Marleeta took the tropical drink and put it on the matching table next to her chair.

"I know, but it's still crazy if you ask me," she insisted.

"Queenie, everybody ain't like you."

"You mean, me and you. Shit, I didn't see you blowing your cash either."

"That's 'cause a nigga like me know how hard it is out in them streets. Cheddar don't come easy."

"I'll drink to that." She raised her glass.

Zack raised his and clinked it against hers. After they sipped, he eased back on the other chair.

"Let's go take a dip when we finish this round," he said.

"Naked again?" She smiled.

"Is there any other way?"

Instead of answering, she reached over and grabbed his crotch. It amazed her at times how she almost passed up this young dick. *I'm so glad I let myself try him,* she thought, knowing her dream life was for real.